A TWELFTH NIGHT MIRACLE

CALLIE LANGRIDGE

Storm
PUBLISHING

Ebook ISBN: 978-1-83700-218-4
Paperback ISBN: 978-1-83700-219-1

Cover design: Tash Webber
Cover images: Unsplash, Shutterstock

Published by Storm Publishing.
For further information, visit:
www.stormpublishing.co

ALSO BY CALLIE LANGRIDGE

For Pete
Thank you for many a Happy Christmas x

PROLOGUE

A woman places a suitcase on a table in a small parlour. She checks she has everything she needs for her trip. She smiles at the gift she has carefully wrapped in yellow paper with yellow ribbons, delighted that her daughter and husband have decided to keep the gender of their imminent arrival a surprise.

She zips up the suitcase and places it on the floor with her handbag, checking her notes on a pad on the desk in the corner. She hates to leave when there is so much to do for the Twelfth Night party, and she should be there to arrange everything. But it can't be helped. Some events are immovable! And she can trust the person who will oversee proceedings in her absence. They are the most trustworthy person she has met in twenty years of working in this house.

When she is happy she has jotted down every instruction that will be needed, she takes a coat from the back of an armchair and shrugs it on. She pulls on gloves and ties a scarf at her neck. She collects her suitcase and handbag, taking a look around the room. It always makes her smile to see the Christmas tree in the corner and the paperchains decorating the ceiling.

Out in the corridor, she puts her suitcase on the floor and opens the door to the outside. She braces herself for the cold

December air but doesn't expect a wind to whip up. It's so strong and so sudden that she is pushed back momentarily. A flurry of dry leaves blows onto the mat. She closes the door and shakes her head. She collects a dustpan and brush from the kitchen to sweep up the leaves. She is about to tip them into the bin when she spots something other than a leaf in the dustpan and fishes it out.

She takes the item through to the parlour. It's a small card, advertising a local business that is offering the type of service that might be of interest. She shrugs and places the card on the desk; she will take a better look when she returns from her trip. She turns to leave but stops at the smell of sweet woodsmoke. She pulls the guard away from the fire. It hasn't been lit in days. She is sure she can hear footsteps and a child's laugh in the corridor. She looks out but there is nobody there. She shrugs again. It's no doubt one of the children of the household playing games. She collects her suitcase and opens the door to the outside.

There is no wind, no leaves, just a crisp winter's day.

ONE

Freya stood in the kitchen at a New Year's Eve party. All around her, people laughed and joked. Dozens of guests filled the kitchen and adjoining living room. Music played. Through the open doors, she watched the other guests dance to a song they all loved. It was a song played at every birthday party and wedding, or any celebration of her group of friends. She clasped her drink, smiling and nodding at the conversation taking place between the group around her as they leant against the kitchen counters. She reminded herself to smile and to laugh at all the right points to show she was joining in. When someone offered her the bottle of wine, she placed her hand over the top of her glass. She pulled a face to indicate that she had already had one too many. Everyone laughed and nodded at her reaction. They clearly thought she was back to her old self. And they were clearly relieved to see it. She was managing to put on a show. What nobody saw was that at every opportunity – and when she was sure she was not being watched – she poured most of each glass of wine down the sink.

Excusing herself, Freya nipped to the tiny downstairs loo. She closed the toilet and sat on the lid. She held her head in her hands, steeling herself to return to the party and to the conversations and the laughter of her friends, many of whom she had known since she attended nursery school. As the years had gone by, their numbers had swelled through senior school and then college. They were the band that celebrated every life event together, the tribe who had supported her through the events of the summer.

Freya dug her fingers into her hair and clutched her scalp. The grief that followed her every day welled in her stomach. They had started to ask less often how she was coping. Six months was probably long enough to look to the future rather than the past. Nobody had said as much, but it felt as though they had. And they were probably right. With time, grief might be expected to morph into something else. Into an aching sadness. But the sharp point of grief had not yet given up on her. It stabbed at her stomach again. Freya clasped her head tighter. If any of her friends on the other side of the closed toilet door had known, they would have rushed to her, held her and cried with her. The life she had lost – the soul that had slipped away on that warm June day – had been known to all of them. Had been loved by them all. For the final year they had provided support and love, along with dishes of food, bags of shopping and a shoulder to cry on as that life drew to its close. They had all wept with her in the pews of the local church and stood beside her at the cemetery. As they would have stood with her now. One word and they would have rushed to her. But she had imposed upon them for long enough. They should be allowed to enjoy their party.

A voice called out that there were just ten minutes to go. The volume of the music rose – Kylie Minogue's 'Spinning Around', a favourite of theirs for so many years – brought whoops and cheers. Freya flushed the loo and washed her hands. Checked her face in the mirror. Took a moment to lean forward, holding the sink and breathing deeply before opening the door. She smiled to her friends who beckoned for her to join them. She mimicked holding a glass, pointing to the kitchen as though she was in search of another wine. They laughed and nodded and returned to their dance. She watched them. Having fun. Singing and laughing. She was usually the first to dance. The first to sing. The first to hold the hands of her friends and lead them in fun.

Freya looked to the kitchen. And then to the front door. She was halfway between each. She could go one way or the other.

Out in the freezing night air, Freya pulled the door gently behind her. Shadows through the closed curtains danced on the stone paving of the front garden. The music followed her down the drive. She wrapped her arms around herself, crossed the street and followed the light of the streetlamps to a cul-de-sac. It took only moments to reach the house in the curve of the street. A neat house. A warm house. The one home Freya could remember clearly.

The only light came from a string of fairy lights on the Christmas tree in the window. Tiny, hazy, multicoloured lights. The only reason Freya had put the tree up was because she knew it's what her grandmother would have wanted. Every Christmas of Freya's life, it had stood proudly in the bay window. Always the real tree Grandma grew in a pot in the back garden and which together they would bring inside and decorate with tinsel while drinking mulled wine and eating gingerbread angels.

But this year, there had been no warming drink, pricked with cloves and orange. No spiced gingerbread angel, pressed from one of Grandma's vast collection of Victorian cookie cutters. This year, there had been no Grandma.

TWO

1ST JANUARY, FOUR DAYS UNTIL TWELFTH NIGHT

'No. No, I'm fine, really... I just felt a bit tired. A bit off colour... Yes, you're probably right. The flu is doing the rounds. No, no, there's no need to come round. I'll be fine. Honestly. Yes. Yes, let's meet for coffee next weekend. I promise, I'm fine. Enjoy your day with the family.'

Freya ended the call and placed her phone down on the kitchen table. It was the fifth call that morning where she had made excuses for her hasty departure from the New Year's party. She hadn't lied to her friends. She *had* felt off colour. Just not for the reasons they thought. And it would only have been a matter of time for the questions to start. How was she really? Why had she spent Christmas alone? Why hadn't she gone to stay with Liam and his family?

Freya folded her arms across her chest and walked around the kitchen. She filled the kettle and put it on to boil. She ran her fingertips along the kitchen counter and straightened a stool beneath it. It was the stool she had stood on as a child to reach the counter, mixing cake batter and weighing out ingredients under Grandma's expert instruction while Liam spent weekends in Grandad's garage, learning all there was to know about the workings of a car.

Crossing the room, Freya leant against the sink. She looked out of the window at the garden stripped of colour by winter. She had been only five years old when she came to live here with Grandma and Grandad. Liam had been eight. She had memories of their mum and dad, but not many. Grandma and Grandad had told them stories of their life before the car accident to make sure they knew how much their mum and dad had loved them, but that's what they had been: stories. Her real life was here. In this house. With Grandma, Grandad and Liam.

Freya focused on a leafless bush in the garden. This always happened. One thought led to another and another, so that she was bombarded by memories held in this house, in everything she looked at and everything she touched. There were days when all she could do was sit at the dining table, poring over the photograph albums Grandma religiously kept, making sure her grandchildren's lives were captured at every opportunity, so they always had memories. Holidays to Cornwall, days out to the seaside, birthday parties, school plays, lazy summer days in the garden, Liam in his Cub Scout uniform, Freya in her Girl Guide uniform, Liam and Grandad with their heads under a car bonnet, Freya in her little apron with a wooden spoon too big for her hand, standing on her stool at the counter, Grandma beside her.

The kettle rumbled to a boil. It clicked to switch off. Freya took a mug and spoon from the draining board and placed them beside the kettle. There was an album of photographs of Liam's wedding to Kate when Freya and been an eighteen-year-old bridesmaid with pink hair and plans to study textile design. There was an album of photographs from her parents' wedding, where her mum looked just like Grandma in the single photo of Grandma and Grandad's own wedding, taken on the steps of a registry office in London – Grandma in a white mini dress with a broad smile, her hair bobbed to her chin; Grandad in a tight suit with a waistcoat and tie, and his hair rather long and much darker than Freya had ever known it. So many times over the years, she had asked her grandparents to tell her the story of how they had met in a nightclub in London. According to Grandad, all the girls had their eyes on him as he used to be a dashing famous racing driver. But in Grandma's version of the story, he had been rather less of a celebrity and only had eyes for her. Whatever the truth of that first meeting, they had been the happiest couple Freya had ever known. They always smiled when they were together.

Freya closed her eyes. She gripped the edge of the counter. She could hardly bear to remember Grandma's grief when Grandad died just a few months after Liam and Kate's wedding and only a few days after they moved away to London, where Liam got the job of his dreams as a mechanic for a motorsport company. Freya had never regretted putting her university plans aside. She had convinced Grandma that her heart lay in a course at the local catering college. She would take books from the library for them to study at the kitchen table while sharing a pot of tea. And together they built a business that saw them in demand for all manner of celebratory cakes with a historical theme. Weddings, birthdays, anniversaries – whatever the occasion, they would produce the very best cakes and bakes from their kitchen. They had catered Tudor parties, historical re-enactment societies, 1920s Great Gatsby parties – all to Freya's designs. Grandma had often joked that she would enter Freya for *The Great British Bake Off*.

Freya pulled out a chair and sat down at the table. All that had come to an end last January when she received the call which made her rush to the hospital. For six months, she had cared for Grandma after the stroke, supported by an army of Grandma's friends who brought casseroles of homemade food, bunches of grapes and sat for hours to chat to Grandma. People still occasion-ally dropped by – but not in the same way.

Freya ran her finger over a familiar knot in the pine tabletop. Would she be able to take this table with her when she left? Because the house had to be sold, with the proceeds split between her and Liam. She would have a deposit to put down on an apartment and Liam would use his half to extend his house in readiness for the third child he was expecting with Kate. In the autumn, he had been to clear the garage of Grandad's tools and car parts and gardening equipment – what Liam had wanted, he had taken, the rest had been sold with the money going to the estate. Freya's part of the bargain was to clear the house. Every cupboard and drawer had to be emptied. Every wardrobe cleared. A decision made on every item – whether it was precious enough to keep or whether its destiny lay in the charity shop. Kate had offered to help, but Freya had always put her off. In the same way she had ignored every call and message from the estate agent wanting to arrange a time to put up the For Sale sign.

A tear slipped down Freya's cheek. She wiped it away on the back of her hand. She lived twenty-four hours a day in a house of memories, but without the people who had made those memories. She had hardly worked in a year. Her savings were running precariously thin. Even with the inheritance, she would have to work to pay a mortgage.

All these thoughts chased each other around her brain. Grandma had always said she should try to slow her thoughts down. *'You go at a million miles an hour. Each of your thoughts is precious. You'll catch yourself on the way back if you're not careful and it's not your responsibility to worry about everything in the world.'*

Another tear slipped down Freya's cheek.

The house phone rang. Freya sat and listened to it. Whoever it was would call back if it was important. The phone stopped. Then rang again. Freya wiped her eyes and grabbed the phone from where it sat beside the kettle.

'Hello,' she said.

'Hello,' a male voice replied. 'Is that Miss Harris of Past Time Bakes?' The man spoke with a soft Scottish accent. It was nobody that Freya knew.

'It is,' she said, switching to business mode. 'Can I help you?'

'I'm sorry for calling you on a holiday,' he said. 'I'm Callum Miller, the estate manager at Hill House. The Mandevilles who own the house are hosting a party and the person who was supposed to be making a cake has had to pull out.'

Freya grabbed the pad and pen kept beside the phone for such calls. 'What's the event and when would it be?'

'It's a Regency-themed Twelfth Night ball on... well, Twelfth Night. We need a Twelfth Night Cake and Regency treats for the fifth of January.'

'*This* fifth of January?' Freya said. 'In four days' time?'

'Anything you can do would help,' Mr Miller said. 'The Mandevilles have forty guests coming to the ball and the cake was supposed to be the centrepiece.'

'But a Twelfth Night Cake is a heavy fruit cake,' Freya said. 'That would usually need to be baked at least a couple of weeks in advance. Then there's the decoration—'

'So, you know what's needed?' Mr Miller said.

'Yes.'

'I appreciate it's very short notice.'

'What treats were you were thinking of?' Freya asked.

'Whatever you think best. The dinner is being catered separately.'

Freya thought for only a few moments. She could hardly look a gift horse in the mouth. 'Is it the Hill House just outside Northampton? Sort of a big country estate? I think I've seen signs for it.'

'That's the one,' he said. 'And we have kitchens here if you need to make use of them.'

'Okay,' Freya said. 'I'll do it. I can't guarantee it will be the best cake I've made but I can make something.'

'That's great news,' he said. 'You come highly recommended. Will I send my details to your website, and you can send me a quote?'

'Of course,' Freya said. 'Send them through and I'll get right back to you, Mr Miller.'

She could hear the smile in his voice when he said, 'Please, call me Callum.'

'If you're sure,' she said. 'And I'd prefer it if you call me Freya.'
'Freya it is,' Callum said. 'Thank you, Freya. You're a lifesaver.'

Callum from Hill House was true to his word and within ten minutes had sent through more details of the party. Freya worked out a quote which Callum agreed, and the deal was done. She would have access to the Hill House kitchens from 3rd January and could arrive at any time.

Sitting down with her laptop and a cup of tea, she clicked through files of recipes, settling on a range of Regency era cakes and biscuits. She looked up the coat of arms of the aristocratic Mandeville family and ideas for the design of the Twelfth Night cake began to take shape. It should be a spectacular confection to impress guests. She could bake the rich fruit cake tomorrow at home and feed it with brandy for a couple of days. It wasn't ideal, but it would work. Then she could transport the cake to Hill House for decoration where she could bake the other sweet treats in the days before the party. Hill House was only ten miles away, on the other side of Northampton, so it would be easy to get there and back each day and she could take all the equipment she needed.

Freya began assembling baking trays, cake tins, pans and bowls, wooden spoons and spatulas. Parchment paper, measuring spoons, piping bags, nozzles, aprons, a set of scales and the Kenwood mixer. When she was happy she had what she needed, she packed everything in large bags. It was only then that she looked to the cupboard where Grandma's collection of historic cookie cutters was stored. It was a collection amassed over decades from charity shops, antique shops and online auctions. Grandma had known instantly if a cutter was old rather than a modern reproduction and had been fastidious in making sure each was food safe.

Opening the door, Freya reached inside. She selected the cutters she would take, wiped them carefully and placed them in a tin. She put the tin in one of the bags and let her hand rest on the top. Had this booking come in at this time last year, she would be standing with Grandma, writing lists and packing equipment, chatting and drinking tea, sharing ideas for recipes.

Freya breathed in sharply and pulled her hand from the tin. So many times, day and night, she was sure she could feel Grandma's presence beside her. It didn't seem possible that a life could simply disappear. Surely there had to be something left. Somewhere.

It was only early afternoon but it was already almost dark outside. In the living room, Freya turned out the main light, sat on the sofa, and took the remote control from the coffee table. Clicking on the television, she pressed play on the DVD that was always in the machine. The opening credits of *Pride and Prejudice* and the jolly title music began to play. Grandma had always insisted that Colin Firth made the best Mr Darcy, and the 1995 BBC version was the best by far. Freya had liked to tease her and say that Matthew Macfadyen was much better. But neither had minded watching either version, along with the many other historic dramas Grandma had amassed on DVD over the years. Whenever a new Sunday night period drama was announced, they had looked forward to it as though looking forward to Christmas. It was their thing. To sit on the sofa together, with a cup of tea and a box of chocolates and watch a period drama.

Freya clutched a cushion and curled into the corner of the sofa. By just the fairy lights of the Christmas tree, she watched the ball begin at Meryton and Mr Darcy look across the room to Lizzie Bennett.

THREE

TWO DAYS UNTIL TWELFTH NIGHT

- Three bags of equipment – check
- Three bags of ingredients – check
- Cool box of ingredients – check
- Kenwood mixer in its bag – check
- Folder of recipes printed out – check
- Notebook – check

Freya rifled through the bags in the back of the car one last time. It was still dark outside, so she had to rely on the interior lights of the car. When she was sure she had everything she needed, she closed the doors with a reassuring thud and slipped the keys into the driver's side lock. Getting inside, she closed the door and shivered, a cloud of breath hanging in the air around her. She pushed the key into the ignition and pulled out the choke, saying a little prayer as she turned the key. The engine whined a little. 'Come on,' Freya coaxed. 'Be a good boy today.'

The car spluttered and the engine rattled to life, like a barrel of rusty spanners. Freya put her foot to the accelerator and pressed gently. The car revved and the engine fell into a rhythm. Freya pushed in the choke and turned on the heater for the windscreen.

It was about as effective as if she'd gone outside to blow on the glass herself.

'*He's an old codger, like me,*' Grandma had explained when she took Freya to see the car that was to become their business transportation. '*And he looks the part for a historic bakers.*' Grandma convinced Freya that the 1963 Morris Minor Traveller in Almond Green, decorated with pale wood down the sides and across the two doors at the back, was just what they needed as it was more like a van than a car. Liam had sucked his teeth and shook his head when he visited to give his opinion on the purchase. He insisted on putting it on a trailer and taking it away to his workshop to do some work on the engine, the brakes and the bodywork. And he was especially eager to install seatbelts. When Liam returned the car, it gleamed, inside and out. He'd even revarnished the wood and had a transfer of their logo made to go on the passenger door, so everyone knew 'Past Time Bakes' were on their way.

Old Morris – the rather unoriginal name he had been christened by Grandma – was a bit temperamental. '*He just needs a bit of encouragement,*' Grandma explained as she revved his engine on days when he complained a bit.

Grandma had been right. Everywhere they went, the sight of Morris made people smile. And Past Time Bakes received many commissions based on his presence at fairs and festivals and celebrations. One little boy had been so enthralled by the old square car that he insisted on having a 'Morris' cake made for his fifth birthday party.

Freya wiped the melting ice from the inside of the windscreen with her cuff. She turned on the headlights and checked her watch. Seven o'clock. Well, she had been told that she could have access to Hill House any time from 3rd January to the day of the party.

Fastening her seatbelt, Freya patted the dashboard. 'Just you and me this morning,' she said. 'Be kind will you, Morris?' She pressed her foot to the accelerator and Morris responded instantly. Putting the car into gear, Freya let off the handbrake and pulled away from the kerb.

The streetlamps were still on, and Freya passed just a few cars as she headed away from town and onto the main road. After a few miles, she passed through the centre of a sprawling housing estate, which she had driven through many times on her way to the motorway. A small precinct of shops sat on one side with a library on the other and a pub on the corner, its sign illuminated from above. The Hill House Arms. It hadn't occurred to her before that the name had any particular relevance.

Carrying on through the estate, Freya passed streets and streets of identical houses, curtains tightly drawn, Christmas lights glowing in a few windows.

Emerging eventually on the far side of town, Freya drove up the bridge crossing over the top of the six lanes of motorway. She took a left at a large roundabout and followed the directions on a map she had printed, turning onto a narrow lane which ran parallel to the motorway. Working in areas with patchy internet, it had always been their way to print maps and instructions rather than rely on phones.

With the hum of fast-moving traffic on the other side of a dense line of trees, Freya followed a high brick wall opposite the trees. There were no buildings on the quiet lane and no other cars going in either direction. A few streetlamps cast only dim pools of light on the lane that seemed like it would lead to nowhere. Freya was about to stop to check the map when the wall came to an abrupt end and gave way to a church, its spire rising high into the dark sky. She was pretty sure there had been a church on the map.

After another short section of brick wall, the lane suddenly ended and Freya brought Morris to a stop. On one side of the lane, a set of steps led up to a footbridge crossing over the motorway, and on the other stood a set of ornate gates. Above the open gates, two golden lions held aloft a globe between them. Freya recognised them from her research. The lions and globe were the coat of arms of the Mandeville family. So, this must be Hill House. She craned to look up to the top of the gates. Golden lions. Beside a motorway and on the edge of a housing estate. It wasn't something you saw every day.

Putting Morris into gear, Freya drove slowly through the gates and found herself on a long drive surrounded by parkland. The day was trying to break, and freezing mist hung over the grass and clung to the trees stretching away as far as she could see. At the end of the drive sat a great white house, which grew larger the closer she drove.

Freya brought the car to a stop outside the house. Large windows lined two floors, with smaller windows up at roof level. A portico with pillars surrounded a huge front door and the white stone of the walls seemed to glitter in the pale morning light. Freya had visited many grand houses in her line of business, but Hill House had to be about the most beautiful. It sat so perfectly in its grounds, nestled amongst trees, with the winter day dawning pink around it. As large as Hill House was, it didn't feel intimidating. It felt like a home. A home somehow set apart from the world just a hundred yards from its gates. And it was hard to believe that it sat just a short way down a lane she had driven past so many times.

Freya steered Morris slowly around the side of the house, his tyres crunching through the gravel as they passed a conservatory. They came to a stop at a set of steps leading down from ground level. All around, the land rolled away to hills, frosty fog clinging to the grass like a hazy blanket.

Freya paused for a moment to take it all in before grabbing her bag from the passenger seat.

An automatic light came on above the staircase as Freya made her way down the stone steps to the basement level. Reaching the bottom, she found a single, half glazed door through which she saw a well-lit long corridor stretching to a set of stairs at the far end leading up. Looking around for a bell, Freya found a metal handle beside the door. It was attached to a sort of pulley above. She took hold of the handle and pulled it down. A bell rang somewhere inside the house. Freya laughed. It wasn't the usual type of door-bell, but a jingling bell. She could picture it on some coiled piece of metal, just like she had seen so many times on Grandma's period dramas.

Almost before the bell finished ringing, a pair of legs emerged from the top of the stairs at the far end of the corridor, taking the steps down two at a time. Freya watched as they became full legs up to the waist and then a man, dressed in dark jeans, a tweed jacket, tweed waistcoat and a checked shirt, open at the neck. He looked like a farmer. He made his way along the corridor, a small dog following close at his heels – a sort of scruffy white terrier with one tan-coloured ear and a tan patch on its back.

The man smiled and gave a wave. Freya raised her hand and waved back. It would have been rude not to. Stopping at the door, the man bent to slide a bolt at the bottom and then slid another bolt across at the top. His waistcoat rode up, making his shirt gape a little, revealing a line of dark hair running down from his navel. With one hand, the man tucked his shirt back into his trousers and with the other, he opened the latch. Freya looked away briefly and fiddled with the strap of her bag.

The door opened and the dog ran out. Before Freya knew what was happening, its paws were on her leg. She stooped and stroked its head. 'Hello,' she said. 'Aren't you friendly.'

'Too friendly, sometimes,' the man said.

Freya stood up. She knew the voice immediately.

'Jasper's just a pup and has a lot to learn about manners, don't you, boy?' The dog ran to the man and stood at his feet. 'Callum,' he said. 'Callum Miller.'

'Freya,' Freya said. 'From Past Time Bakes.'

'I thought as much.' Callum smiled. He pushed his dark hair away from his face. 'It's good to meet you.' He reached out his hand. Freya removed her glove and took his hand. His fingers were warm against hers, his handshake firm. His hands were large and his skin just a little rough, as though he worked outside a great deal.

'Come in and get warm,' Callum said, letting Freya's hand slip from his.

Freya took a step inside and Callum closed the door behind her.

Above them, multi-coloured paperchains interspersed with crepe paper bells zigzagged the entire length of the corridor.

'The volunteers made them,' Callum said. 'They give the place a festive feel.'

Freya nodded. She hoped he didn't hear the sadness in her voice when she said, 'I hope I'm not too early. You said to come anytime this morning.'

'I meant it,' Callum said. 'I'm an early bird myself. The kettle's on if you want a drink.'

'No, I'm okay, thank you,' Freya said.

Callum nodded. 'I'd almost given up on finding a replacement baker.'

'I didn't have anything on,' Freya said.

'Quietened down after the holidays?' Callum said.

'Something like that,' Freya said.

Callum smiled. Up close, Freya saw that his eyes were brown, matching his dark brown hair. Fine lines around his eyes made her think he was maybe just a little older than her. Mid-thirties, perhaps. A little stubble darkened his chin and cheeks. And there was that smile. That friendly smile.

Freya shook her head and looked away. 'Sorry,' she said. 'When you phoned, you said we had come highly recommended. Who was it that recommended us?'

'I found your business card,' Callum said. 'In the housekeeper's parlour. She only keeps the cards of people she wants to use so you must have been recommended to her.' He shrugged and laughed gently. 'Planning parties isn't normally on my job description. I'm just keeping an eye on arrangements as the housekeeper's away for a few weeks while her daughter has a baby. You'll usually find me out on the estate somewhere.'

Freya looked up into his face again. His brown eyes seemed to shine. 'Would you be able to show me where I can set up to work?' she said quickly.

'I've kept you chatting too long,' Callum said.

'No, it's okay. There's just a lot to do and I'd best get started.'

'Will I be expecting someone else to come to help you?' he asked.

'No, it's just me,' Freya said. 'Would you like me to show you the designs for decorating the Twelfth Night cake?'

Callum shook his head. 'It would be lost on me. I'll trust your expertise.' He tapped his hand to his leg and Jasper looked up at him. 'This way,' Callum said. He turned and began walking along the corridor. Freya walked beside him, Jasper trotting on the stone flagged floor between them. The walls were painted a pristine white and many doors led away. One stood open, and inside, Freya saw a huge kitchen with ranges running along the far wall, a vast table in the middle, and windows high up in the basement walls. And like the corridor it was festooned with paperchains.

'That's the main kitchen,' Callum said. 'The fridge is always full. So, help yourself to any food or drink you'd like. The caterers will be in later to start their prep for the party, but they're used to having the household staff around when they're working. You won't be in the way. The family aren't due back until the day of the party, so you won't be disturbing them either.'

Just a short way along the corridor, Callum stopped. He pushed a door open and stepped aside. Freya stepped into the room.

'It's the old pastry room,' Callum said.

Freya looked around. As with the corridor, it was painted a pristine white with stone flagged floors. Wooden shelves lined the walls. Cabinets up to waist height lined three walls and the entire run of cabinets was topped with white marble, as was the table in the middle of the room. A modern cooker stood beside an old-fashioned range. A modern fridge sat to the right of a large stone sink. Like the main kitchen, this smaller room had a window high up in the basement wall at ground level.

'I've been here three years,' Callum said, 'and this is the first time I've seen it used as anything other than a storeroom. You're welcome to make use of any of the equipment in the cupboards,' he said. 'Will I help you bring anything in?'

'No,' Freya said. 'I'm fine. And I'm sure you have enough work to be getting on with, what with the party.'

Callum shook his head and laughed softly. 'There's always more work than it's possible to finish in an old house such as this. The party just means that rather than arranging to clear driveways and manage the ongoing maintenance, I'm called on to festoon the house with ribbons and baubles and candles!' He rose his eyebrows and Freya laughed.

'It all sounds lovely,' she said.

'Would you like me to show you where your handiwork will be displayed for the party?' Callum asked.

'Perhaps later,' Freya said. 'Thank you.'

Callum looked down to Jasper. 'Well, boy,' he said. 'Looks like we should get back to business.' Turning back to Freya, he said. 'The back door is on the latch, so you can come and go as you need to. Just shout if you need anything. Take the stone steps up and you'll be in the staff passageways. Take a right and follow your nose and you'll be out in the hallway. If you can't find me, you've got my mobile number. Just give me a call.'

'I will. Thank you,' Freya said, and followed Callum from the room. He stopped just in the corridor.

'I'll say goodbye for now, Miss Harris,' he said.

'Freya, please, Mr Miller,' Freya said.

'Okay, Freya it is. And I'm Callum.' He looked down to the dog. 'Come on then, Jasper,' he said. 'No rest for the wicked.'

Freya headed away down the corridor. But before she got to the door at the end, she turned to look back, watching Callum take the stone steps up into the house, Jasper at his heels.

FOUR

It took six trips up and down the outside steps, but Freya soon had all her bags and equipment in the old pastry room. With the door ajar, she hung her coat and bag on a hook on the wall. She hoped she hadn't come across as rude when Callum explained that the volunteers had made the paperchains. It was just that seeing them had taken her back to childhood Christmases, sitting at Grandma and Grandad's dining table, threading strips of paper together, looping each one to the next, Liam making a face each time he had to lick the end of the strip to form it into a circle. Grandma kept them supplied with gingerbread, while Grandad stood on the stepladder, crisscrossing the chains along the ceiling from the living room to the dining room. The Christmas tree stood naked in the corner as it was always the final thing in the house to be decorated.

Freya let her forehead rest against her coat hanging on the wall. How was it possible that a good memory made her feel so sad? And yet, it did. It was a memory from a life that was now only a memory.

Closing her eyes, Freya took a deep breath and blew the air out slowly. Work. She was here to work. Turning from the wall, she set her sights on the many bags. She began unpacking the ingredients and equipment, lining everything up on the shelves and work surfaces. Whoever had designed this kitchen had known exactly what they were doing. The marble countertops were perfect for storing goods to keep them fresh and the marble-topped table perfect for the preparation of pastry which needed a cool surface.

Taking up her apron, Freya placed the cord over her head and passed the ties around her, securing them at the waist. It had been good to get dressed that morning in the uniform she and Grandma had created for themselves: white long-sleeved t-shirt, beige loose trousers, white trainers and green apron decorated with their logo. The pale colours didn't show the flour so if they needed to look professional when they were on a job, they could slip off their aprons and still look clean and presentable.

Smoothing down her apron, Freya thought of Callum. From the moment she heard his voice down the line, she had formed an opinion of him. She did it with every new customer who phoned. Based on nothing more than a voice and their order, she tried to work out who they were and what they looked like. She was sometimes vaguely right but mostly wildly wrong in what she pictured. But with Callum, the man before her had been oddly accurate to the picture in her head. But it had been more than that. He had felt familiar somehow. She couldn't put her finger on it. But there was something about him.

Freya laughed gently. It could just be wishful thinking. There was no denying that he was attractive. Very attractive. In a sort of rugged, outdoorsy way. With his tweed and stubble and hair that he had to push away from his brown eyes. His very brown eyes. Freya laughed to herself again. He was probably very happily married to someone else who worked at Hill House, with a brood of children to go along with Jasper the dog.

Taking out her notepad, Freya opened it to her job list. She ran her finger down the list and came to her next task. *Feed the cake.*

She opened the largest tin on the marble counter, the width of a serving platter. Removing the lid, the rich smell of dried fruit and butter escaped. Freya placed the lid to one side and eased back the parchment paper wrapping the huge cake. There was another smell. The brandy she had added to the mixture. She breathed in deeply. By rights, the cake should have been made weeks ago so she could feed it a generous slosh of brandy every day to make it both moist and full of flavour. All she could do was her best in the time she had, so she took up a skewer and a bottle of brandy. The cake was intentionally upside down in the tin and, after pricking a series of holes in its base, Freya drizzled it with brandy from the bottle. Today was all about making icing sculptures for the cake as they needed time to dry out and harden. She would make the rest of the sweet treats over the course of the next few days.

Freya popped the cork back into the bottle and rewrapped the cake. Nestled somewhere inside the cake were a dried pea and a dried bean. The tradition was that whoever found one of them in their slice would be the king and queen for the Twelfth Night party and lead the fun.

She was about to replace the lid when a cold draught whipped about the room. It made the parchment paper tremble and the hairs on her arms stand on end. The door hadn't moved but Freya opened it anyway.

'Hello?' she called.

No answer.

She was returning to the pastry room when another breeze whipped about her. She rubbed her arms. It was an old house, so it was hardly a surprise.

Pressing the lid down firmly on the tin, Freya assembled the ingredients and took her mixer and scales from their bags. She weighed out icing sugar and cracked a handful of eggs to separate the whites from the yolks. Then she halved and squeezed the juice from three lemons. She tipped the icing sugar into the bowl of the mixer, followed by the egg whites and a little of the lemon juice. The whir of the beater in the metal bowl had been a constant in her life for so long that it had become like the soundtrack to her work. She laid a sheet of parchment paper out on a tray and prepared her smallest piping bags with the tiniest nozzles that allowed for intricate work. All the while she listened carefully for the slight change in pitch that told her the icing was ready. The yellow of the lemon juice had been beaten out and when she pinched a little of the mixture between her thumb and forefinger, it had a slightly tacky consistency. She filled a piping bag and covered the bowl with a damp towel to stop the mixture going hard.

With everything ready, Freya set to work piping shapes onto the paper. She preferred to work freehand than to a template. Sometimes it was successful, sometimes it wasn't. But she had learned at catering college to always give it a go.

Filling the piping bag many times and changing the nozzle to create different effects, Freya was immersed in her work, placing tray after tray of completed icing decorations up on the shelves to dry, until at just after ten o'clock, a commotion out in the corridor made her put the piping bag aside and look out of the pastry room.

A small troop of people – at least a dozen – were busy bringing all manner of bags, equipment and packages through the back door and into the corridor.

'Hello there,' one of them called to Freya.

While the others disappeared into the main kitchen, the woman made her way down the corridor. She was tall with fair hair pulled back into a high ponytail. Everyone else wore a uniform of black polo shirt and black trousers but this woman wore a camel coloured long woollen coat over the top of a long black dress. She wore boots with heels that Freya would not have risked wearing in icy weather.

'Hello,' Freya said.

'Noelle,' the woman said. 'Of Noelle's Event Design.' She said the name of her company as though Freya should know it.

'Freya,' Freya said. 'Of Past Time Bakes.'

'Oh,' Noelle said. 'So, you're the baker Callum managed to find at the last minute. I told him I didn't fancy his chances of finding anyone after the original bakers pulled out. I said the housekeeper should have let me find someone in the first place. I mean, it's what I do – bring everything together for an event. And I must have delivered at least two dozen events here. But she wouldn't be told.' She paused and looked Freya up and down. 'Lucky Callum to have found someone at the last minute. So, you had nothing else on? No other commissions at this time of year?'

Freya could hear the edge in Noelle's voice. It was an edge that said she doubted someone like Freya could pull off this job. If she'd been any good, why was she available at the last minute? But Freya had no intention of rising to Noelle's bait. Or the undercurrent of bitchiness coming through loud and clear. 'No,' Freya said. 'I had nothing else on.'

'Hmm,' Noelle said. 'Well, I suppose Callum will be breathing a sigh of relief that there will be something on the cake table.' She went on to say that her staff would be all over the house for the next few days. Cooking in the kitchen. Preparing the ballroom. Dressing the tables. 'So, it will be super busy,' she said. 'But you'll be all right in there.' She glanced past Freya to the pastry room. 'Probably best to keep out of the way.'

'Yes,' Freya said. 'Probably best.' She had no intention of going anywhere near Noelle. 'If you don't mind, I have a lot to get back to.'

'No,' Noelle said. 'You get back to it.'

Noelle spoke like she was giving Freya permission. Without another word, Freya returned to the pastry room. She pushed the door to, so it was barely ajar. She could feel her lip curl as she mentally counted to ten as her grandmother had taught her to do so that she didn't say something she would later regret. She was here to work and causing a scene would never look professional. She had worked on enough events where other businesses were involved to know there were times when everyone rubbed along just fine and other times when there was an explicit or hidden edge of competitiveness. And she had learned years ago to focus on what she had to do rather than be bothered by anyone else. Even so, she didn't need someone like Noelle telling her what to do.

Freya leant against the sink and folded her arms over her chest.

Grandma had always said never to bake in a bad mood. '*Your mood – good or bad – will always come out in the taste of the bake.*'

Freya looked along the icing shapes drying on the shelves. The only person she had to answer to was Callum. He had said she was welcome to help herself to anything she wanted. She wanted a cup of tea, and she didn't need Noelle's permission for that.

In the main kitchen, Freya found a small army of Noelle's staff in their black uniforms with black aprons, peeling and chopping and prepping, but Noelle was nowhere to be seen. They welcomed her warmly and took an interest in what she was doing in the pastry room. She boiled the kettle and took a mug from the cupboard and offered to make a cup for anyone interested. When she asked after Noelle, a woman standing at the table peeling potatoes looked up. She introduced herself as Liz and said, 'She's long gone. You won't see her round here when there's proper work to be done.' She waggled her knife in the air. 'But she'll be back on the day of the party to take all the credit.'

Some of Liz's co-workers laughed. Others nodded their agreement.

Freya sat with the caterers to drink her tea and chat about the great banquet they were preparing for the party. It was as close as they could get to the food that would have been eaten at a Mandeville ball at Hill House in the Regency era – elaborate soups, roast meats and vegetables, pickles and fish.

Tea break over, Freya returned to the pastry room to continue making her decorations for the Twelfth Night cake. At just after twelve o'clock, she piped her final decoration for the morning. It required a great deal of concentration to achieve a filigree style in icing. Placing the tray of decorations up on a shelf, Freya checked those she had finished earlier. She smiled as she gently prised a couple from the parchment paper and they came away intact. There would be a few breakages, there always were, but she had made extra just to be on the safe side.

Happy with her morning's work, Freya sat on a stool at the table and took a plastic container from one of her bags. Removing the lid, she took out a cheese and pickle sandwich. She ate looking out of the window high up in the wall. It had turned into a bright winter's day, but she had been so busy, she hadn't even realised. She plucked an apple from the container and took a bite when again she became aware of a draught. She turned around, planning to push the door to a little, and almost fell off her stool.

'Oh, heavens!' she said with a forced laugh. 'I didn't know anyone was there.'

A young boy stepped into the room. 'I hope I'm not disturbing you,' he said. He was a sweet-faced boy with blond hair that curled about his ears and at his neck. He looked roughly the same age as her twin nephews, so about nine years of age. He wore the most beautiful outfit Freya had ever seen; a pair of what looked like beige breeches with dark boots and a white shirt with a frilled collar. Over the top he wore a jacket of the most splendid scarlet, cut short at the front with a sort of tail at the back. A bit like dress jackets Freya had seen men wear at fancy themed parties.

'You're not disturbing me,' Freya said with another laugh, which she hoped was more friendly. 'I was just surprised. I didn't know anyone was behind me.'

'Sorry about that,' he said, taking another step into the room. He stood at the pastry table. 'What is it you're doing here?' he asked.

Freya almost laughed out loud. The young boy was so confident. And behaved like he belonged in this house. 'I'm making the Twelfth Night cake,' she said. 'I've been creating the decorations all morning.' That would catch him out. No child these days would have the faintest idea what a Twelfth Night cake was.

'The Twelfth Night cake!' the boy said, his eyes wide. 'You're making the Twelfth Night cake!' He began to look around the room with what Freya thought was great excitement. 'And there's a pea and a bean inside?' he said.

'Of course,' Freya laughed. She'd clearly underestimated his knowledge.

'I hope it is me who will be king for the night,' the boy said. 'It's thrilling to be able to tell everyone what they must do!'

'It must be,' Freya said, playing along.

'May I see the cake?' the boy asked.

'Well, that would rather spoil the excitement of seeing it for the first time at the party.'

The boy screwed up his nose. 'Oh, you are right. That would spoil the surprise.' He let out a sigh.

Freya put down her apple and wiped her hands on her apron.

'Would you like a sneak peek?' she asked.

'A what?' the boy said.

'I can show you just one of the decorations, if you like,' Freya said.

Again, the boy's eyes filled with excitement. 'Yes, please!' he said.

Getting up from the stool, Freya went to the shelf. She prised a piped heart from the tray. It had a lacey frill around it. In her open hand, she held it out to him.

He looked down. 'Oh, it's beautiful,' he said. 'How talented you are! I cannot wait to see the finished cake.'

'Take it,' Freya said, offering the heart to him. She had meant it to be kind, but the boy took a step away.

'I cannot,' he said.

'Yes, you can,' Freya said. 'It's a spare.'

He looked from the decoration to Freya. He shook his head. 'I must go now,' he said. 'Mother will wonder where I am.' Without another word, he turned and ran from the room.

'I'm sorry,' Freya called after him. Still with the heart in her hand, she followed him into the corridor. The boy had already gone but she did catch sight of a white blur taking the steps up into the house. Jasper.

Returning to the kitchen, she placed the decoration in her

lunch box. She sat back at the table and took another bite of her apple.

'Great work, Freya,' she said under her breath.

The boy must be a child of one of the caterers in the main kitchen, likely brought along as there was no childcare for him for what was left of the school Christmas holidays. He'd probably been told to sit somewhere and stay quiet, and she had frightened him. He'd probably also been told never to take anything from strangers.

Freya dropped the apple core into the bin and wiped her hands. She'd played dress up with her nephews many times over the years but they usually dressed as an animal or a fireman or one of their favourite cartoon characters. Never in an outfit which made them look like Little Lord Fauntleroy. She wasn't even sure where you would buy an outfit like that. Perhaps the boy was in a show or pantomime somewhere and it was his costume. Or with a parent working in historical catering, it was also possible that it was just how he liked to dress, and they humoured him and his old-fashioned way of speaking. And that was why he knew what a Twelfth Night cake was.

Freya took the heart from her lunch box and bit into the white icing. The surface gave with a reassuring shatter and, even if she did say so herself, it tasted good. Just the right amount of lemon juice in the icing sugar.

FIVE

At five o'clock, Freya stood at the sink washing up the last of her equipment. She looked up at the outside world through the window. It was already dark. All afternoon, she had been half expecting Callum to stop by to see how she was getting on. But the only people she had seen passing the door were the caterers or event staff taking boxes and equipment from their vans parked on the gravel behind the house to prepare the upstairs rooms for the party. All afternoon, delicious savoury smells had floated along from the main kitchen and a few of the caterers had stopped by the pastry room to admire her handiwork and to bring cups of tea. She'd even had an audience to watch after she made a batch of marzipan and used it to cover the fruit cake.

With the icing sculptures drying on the shelves – covered in parchment paper to protect them – and everything prepared for the next day, there was nothing else to do. Freya untied her apron, slipped it over her head and hung it on the hook on the wall. She carefully ripped a sheet from her notebook and began scribbling a note for Callum in case he stopped by later and wondered where she was with the bakes.

She had just written 'Dear Callum' when she felt the hairs on her arms stand on end again, as though another breeze had passed by. She looked up. There, standing in the doorway, was the young boy. She placed her pen down.

'Hello,' she said.

The boy smiled. 'Good evening.'

He crossed the threshold into the kitchen and looked up to the shelves. 'My,' he said, his eyes wide, taking in the decorations. 'You have been busy.'

'I have,' Freya said. 'But the best decorations are hidden.'

'Quite right,' the boy said. 'We would not want to spoil the surprise of seeing the cake revealed at the ball.' He stood in a way she had never seen her nephews stand – very straight, his hands clasped behind his back so that his little chest puffed out. His chin tipped up slightly but not in an arrogant way. He just seemed confident. Grown up for such a young boy. And Freya was glad he had come back. She was afraid she might have frightened him off earlier.

'I think you are very talented,' the boy said.

'I wouldn't say that,' Freya said. 'I would say it has been a lot of practice to get to this stage.'

The boy nodded. Slowly. His brow furrowed, again, in a way that made him seem older than his years. 'We achieve nothing in life worthwhile without practice,' he said. 'We must be always on guard against idleness.'

Freya had to hold in a laugh at the way he spoke. 'I agree,' she said. 'Practice makes perfect.'

The boy's brow furrowed again. 'Practice makes perfect.' He said it as though he had never heard the phrase before. 'I think that you have practiced a great deal,' he said.

Freya was about to ask after the boy's parents as they might be worried where he was when she sensed something in the doorway. She spun around. Without waiting, a girl entered. 'Hello,' the girl said. 'I thought I'd find you in here,' she said to the boy. 'Stan can't resist searching out treats!'

'Hey now,' the boy said. 'You are the same as me. More often than not, you are to be found in the kitchens. Looking to see what treat is to be had.'

The girl raised her eyes to the ceiling before turning to Freya. 'I'm Lenny,' she said.

'Hello, Lenny,' Freya said. The girl couldn't have been more different to the boy. She was dressed in jeans with trainers and a red sweatshirt with a sequin heart on the chest. Her hair was bobbed to her chin with the front held back by a hair slide. She looked about the same age as the boy. And she behaved as Freya would expect a child of her age to. She also brought a wonderful energy into the kitchen.

'Are your parents working here?' Freya asked.

'Mine are,' Lenny said. 'They're upstairs at the moment, sorting stuff out for the party.'

Freya smiled. So, she had been right. These children had been brought along while their parents worked.

The girl tilted her head slightly. 'You're Freya, aren't you?' she said.

'That's right,' Freya said. She could only assume that Callum had told everyone she would be working in the old pastry room. *Callum.* She looked down to the note. At the sight of his name, she had to hold in a smile.

Neither of the children replied and when Freya looked at them, they turned to each other.

'It is her,' Stan said.

Lenny's brow furrowed and she gave her head a little shake.

'But one in, one out,' Stan said.

Again, Lenny shook her head.

'What is it?' Freya asked.

Lenny pointed to the note. 'Callum is a very nice man,' she said.

'He seems to be,' Freya said. There appeared to be another conversation going on between Lenny and Stan – as though they had a secret language. It all felt a bit odd. 'Here,' Freya said, reaching up to one of the trays. If she knew anything about kids, she knew they liked sweets. She eased two icing hearts from the parchment paper and held them out to the children.

'Thank you,' Lenny said, taking them from Freya.

'It's one each,' Freya said.

'I know,' Lenny smiled. She seemed genuine, as though she intended to share. Stan eyed the icing and sucked at his bottom lip. 'We should let you get back to writing your note for Callum,' Lenny said.

Still eyeing the icing heart, Stan said, 'His family work for mine, you know.'

Before Freya could ask what he meant, Lenny looked at him and shook her head again.

'I was sent to tell you that there's a pot of hot chocolate on the stove in the kitchen, Freya,' Lenny said. 'You must try it. It's the best hot chocolate there ever was.' She smiled. 'Anyway, we'll see you later, Freya. And like Stan said, there is always one.' She gave Freya another smile and before Freya knew what was happening, the two children ran from the room. 'Thank you for the icing!' they called as they ran away along the basement corridor.

Freya stood looking at the door for a moment. Well, that had been odd! Like a whirlwind entering the kitchen. She looked out in time to see the soles of Lenny's trainers run up the stairs, a white blur beside her. Stan must have gone ahead, with Jasper following at the rear.

Freya returned to the pastry room. She picked up her pen and looked down at the note. What had Stan meant by saying Callum's family worked for his? Was Stan a member of the Mandeville family? He couldn't be. They were all away and wouldn't be back until the day after tomorrow. It really did feel that she had been at the centre of some kind of joke the children had, though not malicious and not directed to make her feel bad. But what had they meant by 'one in, one out'? Why had Lenny insisted on taking Stan's treat for him? And why had they been sent to tell her to try the hot chocolate in the kitchen? Freya shook her head. Just kids playing games. She looked at the note and wrote:

All done for the day.

See you bright and early in the morning.

Freya

Pulling on her coat, Freya grabbed her bag, turned out the light and closed the door of the pastry room. She had her hand in her bag, fishing for her car keys when she passed the kitchen. She stopped and took a step back. The caterers had clearly finished for the day as the room was empty. The activity of the day replaced by peace. The lights were out but a string of Christmas fairy lights glowed on the chimneybreast above the range. By their white light, she saw steam rising from a pot on the stove. She had nowhere to be. Nobody expecting her. And she had always been a sucker for a hot chocolate.

Freya slipped out of her coat and placed it on the chair closest to the door, along with her bag. She took a cup and saucer from the dresser of crockery running along the wall beside the door. All of the crockery was blue and white and in a pattern she recognised as a willow pattern.

The smell from the pot reached her when she was still a few steps short of the range, the steam like a tendril of warm richness enticing her in. Freya placed the cup and saucer on the table and turned to the stove. Closing her eyes, she breathed in the steam. There was chocolate. And the hint of something else. A spice, perhaps. Collecting the pot, she poured some of the chocolate into her cup. It was so thick that it glugged slowly. After placing the pot back on the stove, Freya took a seat at the table. She picked up the cup. Cradling it in her palms, she lifted it to her lips and took a sip. The taste of velvety chocolate filled her mouth. It was joined by spice. Cinnamon. And perhaps even a little red chilli. She took another sip. The steam swirled about her so that she felt the drink as well as tasted it. Whoever had made this, certainly knew flavour combinations. Still cradling the cup, Freya looked around the kitchen. Illuminated by just the fairy lights with the paper chains blowing slightly in an unseen breeze, this was about the most Christmassy she'd felt all festive season. She looked at the blue and white decoration on the crockery on the dresser. Stylised trees beside plants. A building that looked like a pagoda. A little fence running beside the pagoda. Tendrils of plants around the rim of each plate and saucer and bowl. For a moment, Freya imagined stepping into the image. Were the stylised trees willows as the name of the pattern suggested? Was the water behind the pagoda a lake? Or a stream?

Freya's eyelids grew heavy. She placed the cup back in its saucer and looked into the pattern revealed after drinking the chocolate. It had been warm, so very warm. And the room was warm, so very warm. She closed her eyes. Just for a minute. Just a minute...

SIX

CHRISTMAS EVE, 1812

'Imogen! Imogen! Hurry!' a young woman called. She stood in the doorway of a grand house, snow swirling into the vestibule as she held open the door.

'I'm coming, Rebecca,' a voice called from outside. Within moments another young woman rushed inside. She stamped snow from her fine leather boots. 'Trust us to meet a snowstorm just as we were on our way home.' She laughed, her cheeks pinched pink by the cold. She was followed by servants carrying armfuls of evergreens. Like the young women, their hats and shoulders were covered in snow. The young women held their hands out to a fire roaring in a hearth in the vast hallway, the mantelshelf of which was held on the shoulders of two fauns, one playing a flute, the other a lyre. Other staff appeared to help the young women remove their coats and bonnets.

Imogen and Rebecca were the same height. Both were pretty with delicate features. They had thick dark hair tinged with auburn, neatly held back and pinned in place. Imogen had ringlets before her ears, Rebecca did not. There was much chatter as they joined the staff in decorating the hallway with the evergreen branches and the holly and ivy they had collected. They threaded branches through the bannisters of the huge staircase running up the centre of the hallway. They draped the vast mantelshelf. Red ribbons were tied into the boughs, and candles spread throughout so that the hallway glistened and glimmered.

Imogen and Rebecca stepped back to admire their handiwork and thanked the staff. They retired to the morning room at the very front of the house, with large windows looking out onto the snow-covered land. The walls were decorated with fine green silks adorned with birds, while the curtains and upholstery of the chairs about the room were pink. Fine wooden furniture with turned legs sat beneath the windows and along the walls.

The young women stood before the fireplace.

'Don't the decorations in the hall look marvellous, Imogen?' Rebecca said.

'Indeed, they do, sister,' Imogen said.

'Do you think Mother will consider them up to her standards?' Rebecca asked.

'Mother will approve of anything you do,' Imogen said. 'I on the other hand...'

Rebecca touched her sister's hand. 'It is as well to feign observance to duty, even if you are not in earnest.'

Imogen laughed. 'You feign nothing, sister. You are as dutiful as any daughter ever was. I try my best. Am I not attending all the parties Mother has arranged this Christmas? Have I not agreed to talk to all the men she has lined up to find a match for us? Even the bores who will surely send me to sleep! Have I not agreed to attend Queen Charlotte's ball next year to meet even more potential suitors? But even then, my efforts fall short for our mother.'

Rebecca smiled at her sister. It was a conversation they had shared many times. 'And have you promised to be polite to all the suitors?' Rebecca asked.

'We are not out until we have been presented to the queen,' Imogen said. 'So why must I be polite now?'

Rebecca laughed. 'You are incorrigible! I cannot wait until we are presented at court. It will be marvellous. Father says the new house in London will be finished in the spring. What fun we shall have at the balls and parties. And at the theatre and dances.'

The frown on Imogen's face directly opposed the joy on her sister's. 'Do you not tire of being one of *the twins*,' she said. 'Imogen and Rebecca. Rebecca and Imogen. I sometimes think the world treats us as a confection. It will be the same when we curtsey at court. We are hardly taken seriously. We are the identical sisters who can only be told apart as one has curls and the other does not.'

'We know that we are separate people with independent minds.'

'But that is my point, sister,' Imogen said. She began pacing the room. 'We are not independent. Our mother wants us married off. I sometimes wonder whether she didn't convince Father to invest in a house in London simply so that she can show us off to find the best match who she deems worthy of us.'

'You know Mother means well,' Rebecca said, her tone conciliatory.

Imogen stopped pacing. Her arms came down so that her hands rested on her thighs. 'I know she thinks it is what she must do as our mother,' she said. 'But doesn't it sometimes feel to you as though we are prized heifers being put out to the bull.'

'Imogen!' Rebecca looked to the door as though concerned it might open.

'It is true, sister,' Imogen said. She opened her arms and looked about the room. 'All of this will be Tris's when our father dies. I don't begrudge our brother; he is only a little boy. He had no say in being born. But in being born this is all his birthright. He will be able to choose how he lives. He will inherit all of Father's titles and properties. And either he will decide how we live, or it will be at the will or whim of whatever man we marry. We have no freedom to choose our own future.'

Rebecca reached to take her sister's hand. 'We live in this society,' she said. 'And we must do our best to live a good life within its confines. How else would you have it?'

Imogen sighed. 'That's just it, Rebecca. I don't want to be

confined. A bird is allowed to stretch its wings. Why not us? Tris will have a useful life, if that's what he chooses. He is also free to squander his inheritance if that's what he chooses. But what about us? Can we – as women – not have a useful life? Must we look forward to a future where our only purpose it to adorn the arm of a husband and provide him with a brood of children?'

A commotion sounded in the hallway.

The sisters looked to the door. It opened with force and an older woman entered. 'There you are!' she said.

'Good evening, Mother,' Imogen and Rebecca said.

'It is four o'clock already,' their mother said. 'Your father and brother are waiting in the hall. Come along now. Don't dawdle. Don't you want to see your brother now he is home from school?'

Imogen and Rebecca followed their mother into the hall, where a man and a boy waited before the fireplace.

The boy ran to his sisters. They hugged him and fussed him until their mother intervened and smothered the boy's face with kisses. It was impossible to see his face beneath the peak of a large cap.

Imogen and Rebecca stood aside. When their mother was finished with their brother, a servant stepped towards the fireplace to light the Yule log in the hearth. It was a log that Imogen and Rebecca had chosen and wrapped in hazel twigs, and which would burn all through the festive period until Twelfth Night.

Woodsmoke. Girl Guide camp. Sitting on the ground in a circle around a campfire. Tents behind them. Flames glowing and lighting happy faces. Marshmallows toasting on long sticks.

Freya opened her eyes. She looked around without moving, her chin resting on the backs of her hands, her palms flat on the huge table. In the kitchen lit by fairy lights, paperchains swaying gently above her. Cinnamon and chilli pricking the rich smell of chocolate.

Slowly, Freya lifted her chin from her hands. The willow

pattern cup sat before her. It was the last thing she could remember, drinking the velvety rich hot chocolate. What on earth had that been? A dream. Of course it was a dream. But what a vivid dream.

She breathed in. The scent of woodsmoke was gone. But she could still remember it, from Girl Guide camps. She hadn't thought about that time in her life for years. It had been a happy time. A time of freedom and fun. Is that why she had rustled up a dream of sisters looking for freedom? Because that's what it had been. A dream. Of course. She had watched *Pride and Prejudice* last night. Somehow that had mixed with her memories to make a vivid dream. Perhaps the smell of chocolate had reminded her of marshmallows, which led to memories of Girl Guides, which in turn had mixed with the TV show and a log on a fire. But wrapped in hazel twigs? She had no idea where that had come from.

Freya rubbed her forehead. Thank heavens she was alone. She had never fallen asleep at work before. Callum! She looked to the door. Surely if he had seen her, he would have woken her. She took a breath to compose herself before pushing the chair away from the table. She collected the cup and saucer, washed and dried them and placed them back on the dresser. Shrugging on her coat, she grabbed her bag and hurried from the kitchen to the door to the outside.

SEVEN

ONE DAY UNTIL TWELFTH NIGHT, PRESENT DAY

'Damn. Damn. Damn. Damn!'

Freya ran from her bedroom, zipping up her trousers. Pulling her long-sleeved t-shirt over her head, and her hair still wet from the shower, she raced downstairs and grabbed her phone from where it was charging on the hall stand. She always left it down-stairs so she couldn't hit snooze. But she was sure she had set the alarm last night. Clearly not.

Snatching her coat from the bannister, Freya hooked her bag onto her shoulder. There was still so much to do, and she had planned on being at Hill House by eight o'clock. It was now quarter to eight. Fumbling for her car keys in the bowl on the hall stand, she switched out the light, opened the front door, and stopped in her tracks.

Snow. It lay white and untouched on the lawns and road of the cul-de-sac. The sky was heavy with more to come.

Freya wiped the snow from Morris's windscreen with her sleeve. Turning the key in the lock, she slipped inside and pulled out the choke. After the briefest splutter, the engine turned over. Carefully, very carefully, Freya pulled away from the pavement.

Driving in the wake of a salting lorry on the main road, Freya ran through what she had to do for the day: check the icing decorations had hardened; make the gingerbread; make the mince pies; ice the cake.

On the edge of town beyond which Hill House stood, the snow began to fall again. It was far heavier than at home. And it settled on the unsalted pavements.

By the time Freya crossed the bridge over the motorway, it was difficult to see through the windscreen, even with Morris's wipers on full speed.

Freya took a left at the roundabout and slowed to a crawl. The lane leading to Hill House hadn't been salted and she inched along. Past the church, the snow came down even harder so that it was almost impossible to see beyond the front of the car. When the gold lions above the gates emerged through the snow, Freya let out a sigh. She turned onto the drive, fat flakes swirling about the car. She could hardly make out the trees she had seen yesterday and moved forward in her seat, almost pressing her nose to the windscreen. Morris's wipers whined under the pressure of trying to clear a patch on the glass until finally, Freya picked out smudges of light from the windows of Hill House and used them to make her way along the final stretch of the drive.

Bringing the car to a stop to one side of the front door, Freya pulled on the handbrake and turned the key in the ignition. Morris juddered to a stop. She gave him a pat on the dashboard. 'Well done,' she said. Grabbing her bag, she slammed Morris's door, pulled up her hood and ran around the side of the house, the snow whipping at her face.

Coming to the steps at the back, it was impossible to see the land beyond the gravel path. Freya took the steps down and was at the bottom when... 'Hello!'

She spun around. Callum took the final step down into the small space outside the door, Jasper following him.

'Hello,' Freya said.

The snow continued to fall. It settled on Callum's hair and on the shoulders of his jacket. 'We were just out for a walk before it gets too heavy,' he said. He opened the door and stepped aside to let Freya in first. She wiped her trainers on the mat and the warmth of the basement corridor wrapped around her.

'I'm impressed you made it,' Callum said.

Freya turned to face him. He ruffled his hair and stamped the snow from his boots onto the mat. She left it slightly too long to reply and when he looked at her, he smiled.

'It wasn't as bad where I live,' she said. 'The snow. It wasn't as deep. I parked out the front. I didn't want to risk driving around the back since the snow was getting heavier.'

'That's no problem,' Callum said. 'There'll be nobody else arriving today.'

'What about the caterers?' Freya asked.

'You didn't get my message, did you?' Callum said.

Freya fished in her bag and pulled out her phone. She pressed the button on the side. An empty battery symbol appeared on the screen. 'I don't understand,' she said. 'I had it charging all night. I'm sorry, it's not very professional. You should have been able to get hold of me.'

'No harm done,' Callum said. 'I called everyone to tell them not to come. Heavy snow is forecast here today. If you'd rather come back tomorrow to finish off, that would be fine with me.' He peered through the window in the door to the snow swirling around the steps. 'Although you might want to give it to lunchtime to see if it melts. I don't fancy your chances of getting down the lane at the moment.'

'I really need to get on today to stand a chance of finishing tomorrow,' Freya said. 'I'll stay, if that's all right.'

'Fine by me,' Callum said. 'Will you have a cup of tea first? Or coffee?'

Freya looked up at him. He still had snow on his shoulders. His eyes really were very brown. A little tug of war took place inside her and came down on the side of being sensible. 'Thank you,' she said, 'I would really like that... but I should be getting on. I have a whole day of work ahead of me.'

Callum ran his fingers through his hair. 'I admire your dedication. I'll pop down every so often to see you. It can get a bit lonely down here on your own.'

'I'm sure I'll be fine, but thank you,' Freya said. She looked to the floor before following the stone flags along the corridor into the pastry room. She left the door to the room ajar. In the gap between the door and the frame, she watched Callum pass by, Jasper at his heels. Once they were out of sight, she dropped her bag to the floor, shrugged off her coat and hung it on the hook on the wall. She stood facing the door, eyes closed.

Callum was handsome in the dashing kind of way that heroes were in Grandma's period dramas. Dark hair, with dark stubble, a bit swarthy and rugged in tweeds and brown polished boots. Like a country gentleman. She could imagine him in the 1920s or '30s. Or as some dashing hero in an Edwardian drama set just before the First World War. And she was pretty sure she had a teeny crush on him.

She let her forehead gently bang against the door. She had never been one for falling for someone she hardly knew. Most of the men she had dated had been friends of Liam's or more recently, friends of friends. All of them had been quite nice. Quite decent. She still had a soft spot for a few of them. But none of them had been quite right. She had to hold in a laugh. She knew nothing about Callum except he dressed in an old-fashioned way, often ran his fingers through his dark hair, had the softest Scottish accent and looked at her with his brown eyes. It was a sexy accent. And they were very sexy eyes.

Freya banged her forehead on the door again. Hand on heart, she could say she had never fallen for a client before. She should have accepted that tea. Or coffee. She laughed and shook her head. No, she shouldn't. Grabbing her apron, she slipped it over her head and double tied it at the waist. For all she knew, he was married. Or engaged. Or with someone. Their paths would hardly cross since she was down in the basement. And after tomorrow, she would be gone, moving onto the next job, never to darken the doorstep of Hill House again.

Pushing thoughts of anything other than baking to one side, Freya washed her hands. With great care, she took the trays down from the shelves and was pleased and relieved to find her icing creations had survived the night and everything had set just as she had hoped. She hoicked the mixer up onto the table, laid out her recipe folder, assembled weighing scales, bowls, baking trays and utensils and checked her to-do list.

Freya started by making the filling for the mince pies with dried fruit, sugar, lemon peel and a good slug of brandy, all combined and brought to a bubble in a heavy-bottomed pan. Once the thick, oozing mixture was ready and cooling, she made her pastry in the mixer. She tipped the soft, pale dough onto the marble pastry table. There was something satisfying about using the table for the purpose for which it had been made. Freya smiled as she dusted the surface of the table and the rolling pin with flour. Putting the heels of her hands to the wooden pin, she rolled it backwards and forwards, easing the dough out over the cool surface. She took up an oval cutter and began cutting a regimented line of shapes, butting each one against the next. When she had finished cutting the shapes from the sheet, she pressed the remnants together and rolled it out. 'Waste not, want not' had been drilled into her for as long as she could remember.

When she had used every inch of the pastry she could, Freya cleared down the table and took out a baking tray. Unlike modern mince pies, she had read that traditional pies should be made by taking one of the ovals and adding a spoon of mincemeat before using another oval of the same size to cover the mincemeat and pressing the edges together. After brushing the top of each pie with an egg wash, she put the tray in the oven and started the process all over again to make a second batch. There were lots of mouths to feed at the party. And at Past Time Bakes, they had a rule that there should always be enough for everyone to have two of everything.

. . .

Mince pies were cooling on wire racks running the length of the counters and Freya was putting the fourth batch in the oven when there was a knock at the door. She heard the voice before she saw its owner.

'How's it going?'

Still with her back to the door, Freya took a moment to breathe and to shake away her ridiculous thoughts of earlier.

'Fine, thanks,' she said. But as she turned around the ridiculous thoughts came rushing back. Callum stood there, framed by the wooden surround. He was tall and broad and... yes, dashing. And there was a smile in his voice when he touched the tip of his nose.

'You have a little something...' he said.

'Oh. Oh, right,' Freya said. She swiped at her nose. 'Flour?' she asked.

'It's gone now,' Callum said.

'Occupational hazard,' Freya said, trying to make a joke, to get her ridiculous thoughts to take a break.

'It's worth it,' Callum said.

'Pardon?'

'The occupational hazards. They're worth it when they produce this.' He took a step into the room. 'They look and smell amazing. I've been wanting to stick my head in every time I've been down here this morning. But didn't want to disturb you. You've been busy.'

Freya shrugged.

'I'm guessing you haven't looked outside this morning,' Callum said.

'Not since I arrived,' Freya said.

'Come with me,' Callum said.

Freya took off her apron and placed it on the table. She followed Callum from the pastry room and along the corridor. Callum opened the door to the outside and a blast of icy air whipped about them. He indicated for Freya to go up the steps. Callum followed and stood a couple of steps below her.

'Oh,' Freya said, looking around the landscape. The snow had stopped falling, but while she had been in the basement, the world had turned white. The sun was now shining on a beautiful winter's day.

'It's predicted to start again this afternoon,' Callum said. 'If you left now, you could get down the drive. With it being gravel, it's usually not too bad. If you give me twenty minutes, I can get the truck out and go and salt down to the main road and shovel away anything too deep so you can get through. The main road should be clear. They just don't salt down the small side roads like ours. Especially as there's only a church and one house down here.'

'Do think the party will still go ahead tomorrow?' Freya asked.

'I can't see why not,' Callum said. 'This is all due to melt by the morning. Noelle is coming tomorrow with extra staff. You could come back tomorrow too.'

'But I'll never be able to catch up,' Freya said. 'There's only one of me.'

'That there is,' Callum said. He paused. Freya turned to look at him on the step below. 'Sorry,' he said, shaking his head as though shaking away a thought.

'For what?' Freya asked.

Callum coughed. 'There is an alternative. We would still pay you the full amount even if you can't do everything – it's hardly your fault. But the staff and extra guest rooms in the attic are all made up. The live-ins were supposed to come back today but phoned to say their train can't get through.'

'You're asking me to stay?'

'Only if you want to,' Callum said. 'You don't have to, but the offer's there.'

Freya looked down into Callum's brown eyes. The ridiculous thoughts returned, but she did her best to push them down. It wasn't a proposition – well, at least not that type. It was a business proposal so she could complete the job she had been brought in to do.

'I would hate to take money for work that I hadn't done,' Freya said. 'So, if you're sure it's not an inconvenience...'

'No inconvenience at all,' Callum said. 'Like I say, we have live-in staff and bring in extra when we have a big function. We often have to put staff and extra guests up for the night.' He shivered. 'We should get back inside.'

Freya followed Callum down the steps. At least he had his back to her so couldn't see the colour in her cheeks. He had offered her a room for the night so she could work, like so many other people had stayed over to work. It was not a proposition, despite what her mind was trying to tell her. Along with trying to tell her that his eyes seemed to get a little darker when he spoke to her.

At the bottom of the steps, Freya copied Callum and stamped the snow from her trainers. Inside, Callum made to close the door. It stuck and he had to give it an extra shove. 'It swells in the damp weather,' he said to the door. 'I should get that seen to.' Turning to Freya, he said. 'Have you eaten lunch?'

She shook her head.

'Help yourself to anything in the kitchen,' he said.

'Thank you. That's really kind.'

'Think nothing of it,' Callum said. 'The old housekeeper's parlour is in there.' He pointed to the room closest to the door to the outside. 'Feel free to make use of it. Right, I should be getting on. There's so much to do. But the festive season is the best time of the year, don't you think? Especially when we can extend it like this to Twelfth Night.'

Freya thought back to her festive season. To the Christmas lunch of a sandwich and crisps. To the invitations she had turned down. And to the party she had run from before the countdown to bring in the New Year. She tried to smile her agreement. It worked, because Callum continued in the same vein.

'There's an energy to the house at this time of year,' he said.

Freya smiled and nodded again.

'Sorry,' Callum said. 'I'm keeping you talking when you want to get on.'

'It's okay,' Freya said. 'I'm just happy to be here.'

Callum smiled. 'I'll see you later, Freya,' he said. He whistled and Jasper appeared from the kitchen.

Determined not to watch him go up the stairs again, Freya dipped into the pastry room. She listened to his footsteps until they disappeared up the stairs and into the house. *I'm just happy to be here!* Of everything she could have said, why had she said that? Would Callum really care if she was happy to be there? She should have just thanked him for the offer of food and left it at that.

Freya grabbed her oven gloves and took the latest batch of mince pies from the oven. Placing the tray on the side, she used a spatula to move each pie onto a wire cooling rack. She was clearly losing it. For months she had barely left the house. And here she was, falling for a man she hardly knew. Scratch that, she was falling for a man she didn't know at all. In her mind's eye, she saw the flash of navel she had caught when Callum opened the door to her the day before. She swallowed down hard. She had clearly forgotten how to behave around people. Poor Callum. The last thing he needed was the hired help fawning all over him. She shouldn't have accepted his offer to stay. What had she been thinking? But she was caught. If she hadn't agreed to stay, there was no way she could complete the commission. And he seemed to love the festivities. If she saw him again, would she have to pretend to share his enthusiasm or risk offending him?

With the final mince pie of the batch on the rack, Freya's stomach growled. She abandoned the pastry room, went through to the main kitchen, and opened the fridge. She made a cheese sandwich and sat alone at the vast table to eat it, watching the world through the high basement window. It had started to snow again, and a thick layer sat on the path she could see through the top of the window. When she had finished her lunch, she made a cup of coffee. She made a detour to the pastry room to grab her file before heading to the housekeeper's parlour.

Just one step inside the room beside the back door and Freya felt instantly at home. The paperchains from the basement corridor continued into the parlour, crisscrossing the ceiling above her head. There was a small dining table with a neatly ironed table-cloth along the far wall, beside a desk containing files and ledgers. Two red candles decorated either end of the mantelshelf, the base of each decorated with a sprig of holly. A carriage clock ticked in the centre of the mantelshelf and on either side of it sat blue and white pottery dogs, each wearing a little scarf of silver tinsel. On a tall table in the corner of the room sat a small Christmas tree in a bucket decorated with crepe paper. A string of multicoloured lights in the shape of old-fashioned lanterns decorated the branches, along with strands of silver lametta.

Freya placed her file and coffee on a small table and took a seat in one of the two armchairs on either side of the fireplace. The scent of pine filled the air, and Freya watched the lametta twinkle in the light of the lanterns. This was precisely the type of room her grandmother would have loved. Homely, she would have called it. In another time, Grandma would have sat in the chair on the other side of the hearth. They would have chatted over their lunchtime sandwich, discussing what bakes they would make that afternoon. They would have worked side by side at the marble table in the pastry room. They would have sat next to each other in Morris travelling to and from Hill House. And they would have spent the evenings watching a period drama to unwind and for inspiration.

Freya put her hand to her mouth. Every chair next to her was empty now. She stood alone when she worked. She travelled alone and lived alone. Was this how it would always be? She couldn't see a time when she wouldn't be alone. When life wouldn't be empty.

Freya picked up her cup and took a sip of coffee. The saucer rattled when she shakily replaced the cup. She closed her eyes. The carriage clock continued to tick rhythmically on the mantelshelf. The room was warm. The chair soft, so... soft. She could rest her eyes. Just for a few seconds. But she couldn't risk falling asleep. Not again...

EIGHT

2ND JANUARY 1813

Imogen sat beside her sister Rebecca at a large table in a panelled dining room. Festive greenery decorated the mantelshelf and a fire blazed in the hearth below. At least a dozen people were sitting around a long table all dressed in their finery. Women wore dresses pinched in just below the chest with the swell of their busts above. Some wore feathers in their hair. Others wore jewellery that shimmered in the light from so many candles lining the table. The men wore high collars, waistcoats and jackets with long tails. Staff in powdered wigs and uniforms of blue with gold braid served a course of roasted meat. It would seem that no expense had been spared for the array of fine food and wine on the table.

'And how was your Christmas?' Imogen and Rebecca's mother asked from the end of the table. She wore a dark green dress and had a black feather in her hair, which was held back in a tortoiseshell comb. She directed her question to a woman of a similar age just a little way along the table.

'It was wonderful to have all of the children home,' the other woman said. She looked to a young man and young woman who nodded at her. They bore enough of a resemblance with their thick dark hair and fine features to be her son and daughter. Opposite her sat a man in conversation with two other older men at the table; he paid the women's conversation no mind.

'I'm sure it was a delight to have Tris back from school,' another older woman said. She wore a blue dress with a blue feather in her hair. 'He really is a pet.'

Imogen and Rebecca's mother fanned her face. 'I have never known a boy to be in possession of so much energy and be in want of constant entertainment. He is too old to be in the nursery now, but he seems to like it. And I am sure he is keeping the maids very busy up there.'

The other older women nodded.

'I can indeed sympathise with you,' the second older woman said. 'Emily was such a quiet and considered child.' She looked to a young woman, who smiled. 'Arthur, on the other hand, never gave me a moment's peace. He ran the household ragged with his charging up and down corridors and in and out of rooms. Although you would not know it to look at him now, doesn't he look a picture of calm?'

She turned to a young man. Like the older men, he wore a high collar. His waistcoat was cream and his jacket blue. With blond hair and blue eyes, he was immensely handsome. He took a sip of his wine.

'My husband tells me that university brings out the boisterousness in young men. Is that not right, husband?' the woman said.

A portly man across the table paused in his conversation. He nodded his agreement although it was clear he had not heard what his wife said.

'It has had quite the opposite effect on my son,' the woman said. 'Arthur is now more serious than he was. Is that not true, Arthur?'

The young man took another sip of wine. 'I am sure my father would think the money he pays to send me to Cambridge squandered if I spent my time in beer shops rather than libraries.'

Arthur's mother laughed. 'What a serious man my boy has

grown into. Who now talks of joining the clergy rather than the military. Whoever would have thought!'

The three mothers at the table began a discussion on the careers of their grown sons and the prospective matches of their daughters. Their husbands continued their conversation unless called upon to add confirmation of something their wives said. Their thoughts and opinions were neither requested nor given.

Most of the offspring of the three couples followed the various conversations of their parents and spoke when appropriate. What the mothers, fathers and siblings failed to see were the looks that passed across the table between Arthur Richmond and Imogen. When they believed they were not being watched, they smiled at each other. When they believed they were being watched, they nodded in an attempt to show they were listening to the conversations. When more wine was served, Arthur held his glass up to Imogen and she smiled at him. They did not notice Imogen's mother look up at that moment. She saw the look that her daughter and Arthur Richmond shared. The expression on her face changed in an instant from that of a genial hostess to one of anger. It lasted only a moment; she was an experienced hostess and knew what her guests expected of her.

But for every sentence she shared with her guests, she stared at her daughter and the man that had her enthralled.

After the meal, the family stood in the grand hallway and bid farewell as their guests donned coats and hats, saying how very much they were looking forward to the ball in a couple of days. It was the highlight of the season. As the guests departed in their carriages, Imogen's mother said she would like to see her. At once.

'Close the door,' Imogen's mother said when her daughter followed her into the morning room. The older woman paced before the fireplace, the dark expression on her face in stark contrast to the flames in the fire and the shine of the greenery on the mantelshelf above.

The younger woman stood and watched her mother.

The older woman came to a sudden stop. 'You will not encourage this any longer,' she said.

The edges of Imogen's lips puckered in confusion. 'Encourage what, Mother?' she asked.

'You no doubt think you were not seen,' Imogen's mother said.

'Seen doing what?'

Her mother began pacing again. 'You and Rebecca are to be presented this year. The new house will be finished in the spring, and we will travel to London for the season then. Any attachment you think you may have formed in any other direction can be put out of your mind. Now.'

Imogen looked to the floor.

'Have you nothing to say for yourself?' her mother asked.

Imogen continued to stare at the floor.

'A country parson!' her mother said, pacing furiously. 'Is that the husband you aspire to? Well, I can tell you now, that is not what I – or your father – will allow.' She paused to glare at her daughter. She began pacing again. 'Had I known of these... these... feelings you think you have formed, I should never have invited them this evening. And I would certainly not have invited them to the Twelfth Night ball. But there, an invitation once given cannot be retracted without causing offence.'

'But the Richmonds are your great friends. They come to all your dinners and parties. And I have known Arthur and Emily since we were all children. I—'

Her mother came to an abrupt halt. 'Arthur, is it? Arthur! He is Mr Richmond to you. And that is all he shall ever be. I knew I had allowed you and your sister too much freedom. I should have kept a tighter control. Well, from now on, you do not leave this house, you do not speak to anyone, without me or a chaperone that I have appointed. Am I making myself understood?'

Imogen nodded.

'Can you not see that I am doing this for you? You are to be presented. *Presented*. Do you know what an honour that is and the great deal of effort to which your father has gone to provide you with the very best opportunities? Being presented and being out for the season may see you make a match with a noble man or royalty. You would not thank me if I let you settle for a country parson. Oh, you might think yourself happy for a year or two, but then you would come to regret it. And you would be shackled to a life of duty in a draughty country rectory when you could live a far, far better life.'

Imogen nodded. She wore a look of utter defeat.

'There,' her mother said. 'I can see that you understand. These infatuations never last. I think you forget that I was once a girl like you. I understand these things. Now, let us return to your father and Rebecca. And say no more on the subject.'

'No, Mother,' Imogen said.

Her mother did not see the tear her daughter wiped away as she followed her from the room.

The next day, Imogen stood at the head of the stairs. It was after breakfast and her family had begun their business for the day. Father had taken Tris to visit some of the tenant farmers, Rebecca was talking to their maid about how she would like her hair for the Twelfth Night ball, Mother was with the housekeeper and cook scrutinising the menu so not a single detail was left to chance.

The clock at the back of the hallway chimed eleven o'clock. The servants had finished clearing the dining room of breakfast things. Other servants were busy in rooms and had begun their cleaning for the day. Imogen ran down the stairs, across the hall, and let herself out, closing the front door gently behind her.

She ran down the drive, using the cover of trees to hide. Every so often, she looked over her shoulder, but nobody appeared at the door. Finally, she plunged deep into the trees and followed a path through the snow to a gate in a low wall. She entered a graveyard. Saying a silent prayer for all the souls she passed, she came to the door of the church, which was always open. She pushed the great wooden door, and it creaked on its hinges.

It was as cold in the church as it was outside. Imogen closed the door and walked slowly down the aisle past the rows of pews. She had known this place her whole life. Every Sunday she had worshipped here with her family. Many weddings had taken place here. And baptisms. And Easter services. And... She paused. And funerals. In her seventeen years she had paid her respects at many. For members of their household. For friends from the village. For their extended family. But it was the memory of the funeral six months earlier that made her grasp for the support of one of the pews. The pale stone of the floor, hewn to dips by so many feet passing across it over the years, came into and out of focus.

Imogen made her way by moving her grip from one pew end to the next. She reached the very first pew before the altar and collapsed onto the hard seat. At first, she stared at the stone between her feet, until she found the courage to lift her head to look at the brass plaque mounted to the pillar before her. It was set above her family's vault and beside plaques commemorating so many members of her family. She was related to or descended from all of them but had known only two in person – her grandfather and her father's younger brother – until six months earlier, when the new plaque was added.

She stared at that plaque.

To Lady Sophia. Late of this parish. Who did works of great charity and was admired by all, especially those whom she helped. All who knew her wish her eternal peace.

A tear slipped down Imogen's cheek. She did not wipe it away. It was joined by a second. And a third.

She reached into the pocket of her dress and pulled out a small, oval portrait. It had been painted only two years earlier. And was a good likeness of the woman Imogen had known and loved so very much. Her dear grandmother, Lady Sophia.

'I miss you,' Imogen said, holding the likeness tight. 'You and you alone wanted what was best for me.' She wiped away a tear. 'If you were here, you would help me. You would advise me. And I know you would not stand for my mother's unkindness.'

Imogen paused and closed her eyes for a moment, before opening them again to look on her grandmother.

'I'm sorry. I know that was not kind. I know that my mother believes what she is doing – making me go to London – is for the best. But it is not. I wish I'd had these feelings for Arthur when you were here. But they have come on in the last few months. He has always been just a friend since we were small but now... now, he is so much more. We talk so much and share so many of the same desires to do good in the world. As you did. If my mother has her way, I will have to put him aside. My heart will break. As it broke when I lost you. I cannot lose both you and Arthur within the space of just half a year.'

Another tear fell. It landed on the face in the portrait. 'I am lost without your guidance, Grandmama. I am lost without you.'

NINE

PRESENT DAY

Freya opened her eyes. Her head rested against the back of the chair. She stared at the strands of lametta shimmering in the light of the lanterns. The clock on the mantelshelf ticked rhythmically. A tear fell down her cheek and she wiped it away. She picked up her coffee and put it down without taking a sip. These people she had brought into the world through her dreams might only be figments of her imagination, but she could feel Imogen's pain. She too was lost without her grandmother. And Freya didn't even have an Arthur Richmond to hang her hopes on.

Freya sniffed and shook her head, picking up her file. She couldn't do this now. She couldn't fall into the depths of sadness that usually saw her curled on the sofa at home with just the television for company. These dreams were simply her subconscious playing out her sadness in a fictional stately home. It was hardly a surprise as she was in a real stately home. But she couldn't keep falling asleep. Even if Hill House felt safe and warm and welcoming.

Flicking through the papers in the file, Freya began to make mental notes. *Gingerbread. Marzipan cake. Biscuits.* These were all still to be made. Tomorrow she would decorate the cake. Today she would ice the cake. She sorted the printed recipes into order, so they were at the front of the file, which also contained printouts from previous jobs. She flicked through them in case she had missed any pages. Coming to the end, she found a piece of paper that didn't look like any of the others. She pulled it free. It was an application form. Freya read the information in the boxes. It was an application to be a contestant on *The Great British Bake Off*. She had watched it religiously with Grandma. They assessed each bake. What they would have done for the challenge and what they might have done differently. But she'd had no idea that Grandma was applying to be a contest on the GBBO. She read further. And when she came to a section asking why the applicant should be considered to be part of the show, she stopped.

Freya went through so much in her young life. More than any child should ever have to bear. She was lost and together we found baking. It was a language we could both understand. And it helped us both deal with our grief when we lost her darling parents and then my husband, who was the love of my life. Freya and I became a little team. And we still are. I couldn't have wished for a better teammate, workmate and granddaughter. She is both passionate and compassionate and would make a wonderful addition to the GBBO tent. She is a ray of sunshine on the darkest days. You really would be very lucky to have her, as I have been.

The words blurred through Freya's tears. A sob caught in her throat. She had never seen those words before. She had never heard them, but she could hear them now. In Grandma's voice, as though she was standing beside her. She clutched the sheet of paper then released it, afraid she might tear it. With great care she placed it on top of the file on the table before fishing in her pocket. She pulled out a folded tissue and her phone, which was on silent as it always was when she worked. She wiped her eyes. A notification for a message flashed on the screen. She opened it. And immediately wished she hadn't.

Hi Miss Harris, we've been trying to contact you, but you must have missed our messages. We plan on visiting tomorrow to install the For Sale sign in the front garden. We don't need anything from you but wanted to make you aware. Kind regards, Chris Marks, Holroyd's

Freya dropped her phone on the table. Resting her elbows on the arms of the chair, she held her head in her hands. She had known it was coming. Liam had instructed the estate agent before Christmas. He had arranged for photos to be taken when Freya was out so the house could be advertised. Liam had consulted her on everything, but as she hadn't been involved, she had been able to pretend it wasn't happening. But there it was. In the message. Her home was for sale.

A knock came at the door. It opened before Freya had the chance to compose herself. She jumped to her feet and rubbed her eyes with the heels of her hands.

'Hello there,' Callum said. His voice was light and bright but then took on an edge of concern. 'Are you all right?' he asked.

'I'm fine. Fine,' Freya said, but even she could hear the catch in her voice. 'Sorry, I just woke up. I fell asleep.'

'There's no harm in that,' Callum said.

Freya wiped her eyes again. 'The hot air in the kitchen gives me dry eyes sometimes,' she said. It sounded as lame as she knew it was, but she had to say something. 'Did you want me?' she asked.

'I can come back later,' Callum said.

'No, please,' Freya said. 'I've finished my lunch break.'

Callum pushed his hands into the pockets of his trousers and rocked back on his heels. 'I know you're busy,' he said. 'But I wondered whether you wanted to have a look around the house?'

'That would be great, thank you,' Freya said, leaping at the opportunity for a distraction. She could clear her head and be in a better frame of mind to return to her bakes.

Callum smiled, making creases appear around his eyes. 'Follow me,' he said, nodding to the door.

Freya walked beside Callum along the basement corridor. At the end, he stepped aside for her to go up the stone steps leading to a long, thin corridor of whitewashed walls lit by unshaded bulbs. 'This is the staff passageway,' Callum said.

Freya looked up to a row of bells high on the wall, all with the name of a room painted onto a plaque above, she read a few: *Billiard Room. Morning Room. Dining Room.*

'They would have rung all through the day a hundred years ago,' Callum said. 'Some of them still work, but mostly they don't. The current baronet has a mind to have them fixed. Not for summoning staff – there are only few of us now anyway – but to maintain the authenticity of the old place. He's big on restoration.' Callum pointed to the left. 'The staircase at the end there gives staff access to all the floors above. But this is where the tour continues.' He indicated for Freya to take a right along the corridor. They came to a door at the end. 'Are you ready?' Callum asked. Freya looked over her shoulder at him.

'Yes,' she said. It seemed an awful lot of ceremony to open a door to look at a house.

'After you,' Callum said.

Taking hold of the handle, Freya pushed the door open. She stepped through. And stopped.

Before her was a grand hallway panelled in pale wood, with recesses containing pure white marble busts and mythical creatures on plinths. The walls were hung with paintings. Men in powdered wigs, women in fine silk gowns, children in groups, playing with toys. Many of the paintings included animals: dogs, rabbits, cats.

Callum followed Freya and stood beside her. 'What do you think?' he asked.

Freya continued to look around.

'It does leave a lot of people speechless,' Callum said. He started to walk up the hallway towards the front door. He was right; she was speechless, but not for the reason he thought. She looked down at the floor as she followed him – a floor of white mosaics decorated with stylised bronze flowers. Callum came to a stop at the bottom of the vast staircase leading to the floor above, its bannisters decorated with carved animals, birds and flowers. It was carpeted in scarlet with pineapples forming the newel posts. All around, doors led away to many rooms. And to the right of the staircase was a fireplace, the mantelshelf held up by two fauns, one playing a flute, the other a lyre. Above a mirror on the chimney-breast two lions carved into stone held a globe between them. It was the coat of arms of the Mandevilles.

Freya almost didn't know where to look. She knew each detail of this hallway. But how? She had never been here before. Never seen it.

'Has Hill House been used for filming?' Freya asked. It was the only logical explanation for how her brain had used it as a back-drop for a dream about two sisters.

'Not while I've been here,' Callum said. 'But it's possible it was in the past. The Mandevilles are very inventive at finding ways to make money to keep the house and estate going.'

Freya turned to look at the vestibule and the great front door beyond. It *must* have been used for filming. She *must* have seen it in one of Grandma's period dramas. But even that didn't explain how she knew it in such minute detail. Especially as a film set would have been dressed with props. It would not look precisely as it did in its normal life.

The Christmas decorations were similar to those she had seen in her dreams – great swathes of evergreen on the mantelshelf and wound round the handrails of the bannisters, interspersed with red ribbons and strings of dried orange slices. The air was full of the scent of the citrus fruit. As well as the scent of woodsmoke from the huge log aflame in the grate. Apart from the Christmas tree beside the fireplace everything was as she had seen it. This was Imogen's home.

'Feel free to look into any of the rooms while you're here,' Callum said. 'The family open it to the public for events throughout the year and decamp to some of the upstairs rooms. But now the Christmas season is over, this is just their family home again.'

'Thank you,' Freya said. Although she was sure she already knew what she would see in some of the rooms.

'We've tried to stay true to the Regency era with the decorations,' Callum said. 'The evergreens were collected from the estate, and the volunteers put them up. They've done a great job with the ribbons and dried oranges.'

'And the log in the fireplace will burn throughout the festive season and is decorated with hazel twigs?' Freya said.

Callum looked down at her and raised his eyebrows. 'You do know your Regency traditions,' he said. 'The only things that aren't authentic are that Christmas tree and the tree in the morning room. But the current Mandeville children would have been a bit disappointed if they didn't have something to put their Christmas presents under.'

Freya glanced through the open door of the morning room. Again, it looked familiar even if the furniture was more modern and a Christmas tree stood beside the fireplace.

'Right,' Callum said, 'I should show you where the ball will be. It will no doubt spill out into the hallway – they usually do, but the main party will be through here.'

Freya followed Callum to a set of impressive looking double doors at the bottom of the staircase. He took hold of the handles and pushed the doors wide.

Stepping inside, Freya felt her mouth fall open. The hallway was beautiful, but the grandeur of this room took her breath away. It seemed to run the entire length of the house. Gold mouldings decorated the top edges of the room, extending onto the ceiling and down the walls. Two huge fireplaces sat at either end with gold mouldings to match the walls and ceiling. The wall opposite had sets of doors leading out to the grounds of Hill House and were dressed with the longest blue curtains in the richest fabric Freya had ever seen. Above the pale wooden floor hung two huge chandeliers, their crystal drops glistening in the light. It was made almost magical by the snow laying deep outside the doors, giving the whole room a sort of blue-silver tint.

'It's the ballroom,' Callum said over her shoulder.

Freya turned around.

'It's a bit of a surprise in a house this size,' Callum said. 'Apparently, the original baronet was eager not to be outdone by his Caxton cousins across the valley. Have you been to Caxton Hall?' he asked.

Freya shook her head.

'It's magnificent,' Callum said. 'Probably ten times the size of Hill House and much older. It's got some interesting history with a very bad heir a few decades ago. He got into all sorts of trouble and took a dislike to the Mandevilles. He had spells in prison in India and up in Scotland. They don't generally cover him on their visitor tours.' He leant in closer to Freya. 'But for all Caxton Hall's splendour, I prefer Hill House. There's something special about this place. It has a feeling about it I've never experienced in any of the other houses I've worked in.'

'You've worked in a lot of houses?' Freya asked.

'A few,' Callum said. 'But none had the same kind of feeling.' He paused as though thinking about how to explain what he meant. 'It's as though this place has a soul.' He laughed softly. 'I know that sounds ridiculous. But when I'm here on my own, I never feel alone. Not in an odd or eerie way. It feels warm.'

'I don't think that's ridiculous,' Freya said. She thought about the house on the cul-de-sac, and its rooms that she knew inch by inch. She knew every item of furniture. Every knick-knack. Every photograph in every frame. Every plant in the garden and in the pots on the drive.

'Are you all right?' Callum asked.

'Sorry,' Freya said.

'You were miles away,' Callum said.

Freya shook her head, attempting to shake some sense into it. 'I should get on with my work,' she said. 'There's so much to do.'

There was a pause before Callum said, 'I hope I'm not speaking out of turn. But you seem very distracted. We're kind of stuck here together for the time being. If you want, we could have a cup of tea. I'm a good listener.'

'I'm fine, thank you.' Freya looked up into his brown eyes and looked away. He was paying her to bake some cakes. Listening to her woes wasn't part of the deal. Neither was being an object of fancy for her. Professional, she should be professional. In a more confident tone, she said, 'I've had a lot on my mind recently. But nothing that will get in the way of my work.'

'I didn't imagine it would,' Callum said. He smiled, such a friendly and reassuring smile. 'But if you fancy a cuppa then I've been told I don't make a half-bad brew.'

It was Freya's turn to smile now. 'Thank you,' she said. 'I might take you up on the offer later.'

'You do that,' Callum said. 'So, we should be getting you back to the kitchen and I have a to do list as long as my arm to be getting on with for tomorrow.'

'I can find my own way back down,' Freya said.

'It's okay,' Callum said. 'I need to go down to the cellar to bring up some wine for the party, so I'll tag along, if you don't mind.'

'I don't mind at all,' Freya said.

Together they left the ballroom. Callum closed the doors behind them. They passed across the bottom of the staircase and were halfway back up the hallway when Callum stopped. Freya stopped beside him. He pointed to a life-sized portrait hung below the stairs. 'It wouldn't do to have a tour of the house without saying hello to our hero,' Callum said. 'Meet Captain Thomas Mandeville.'

Freya looked up at the painting of a man in military uniform sitting on the back of a black horse, whose coat seemed to gleam in the light. The man wore a blue uniform with red panels at the chest and long highly-polished black boots. He sat proudly in the saddle, a sword by his side and Hill House on a hill behind him. The plume of his golden helmet blew in a breeze. There was so much movement in the painting that it seemed almost alive.

'Why is he a hero?' Freya asked, looking into the man's handsome face and his blue eyes.

'Captain Thomas died in the opening days of the First World War,' Callum said. 'He was shot and killed protecting the men under his command. There are lots of accounts in the archive from the men of his troop that recount the bravery of Captain Thomas and a corporal when they charged the enemy, drawing fire onto themselves. Captain Thomas is not just our hero, he's a hero to the descendants of the men he saved. Many of them visit regularly and some of them are even invited to the ball tomorrow. They are great friends of the Mandevilles.'

'That's wonderful,' Freya said, still looking into the blue eyes. 'To leave such a legacy and be remembered all these years later.'

She felt Callum nod beside her. 'It's all any of us can hope for,' he said. 'To be remembered for the good we did in life.'

Freya felt a tear spring to her eye. She tried to make a noise to say she agreed. She was sure that Callum saw her wipe away the tear, but he didn't say anything.

After a moment or two, he said, 'Ready?'

Freya nodded. She fell into step beside him. She stared at the bronze flower mosaic floor tiles, until they reached a long-cased clock at the end of the hallway beside the door at the back. When she looked up, she saw a ball of greenery she hadn't noticed on their way in. It hung from the ceiling above the door and was about twice the size of a football and formed from tendrils of plants and decorated with red ribbons.

'Another Regency tradition recreated by the volunteers,' Callum said. 'It's a ball of mistletoe. You wouldn't have seen it upstairs in a house in the 1800s. It would have been considered a bit racy and would only have been found in staff areas. But the current Mandevilles don't mind. Stealing a kiss under a kissing bough isn't frowned upon these days.'

Callum's tone softened as he spoke. Freya looked from the kissing bough to him. He held her gaze for a moment before holding out his hand, indicating for her to go through the door that would take them back to the staff passageway.

TEN

Freya stopped beside Callum at the pastry room. He closed his eyes and breathed in deeply. 'The smells coming from in there are wonderful,' he said. 'It's been making my mouth water all morning.'

'Would you like to try a pie?' Freya asked. 'I always make extra so there's plenty.'

'I have never knowingly turned down a baked good,' Callum said. He waggled his eyebrows, making Freya laugh.

Callum followed her into the kitchen and Freya removed the tea towels covering the pies. 'Pick whichever you fancy,' she said.

Leaning forward, Callum looked along the rows of pies as though choosing a precious gem. 'Decisions, decisions,' he said, tapping his top lip with his forefinger. Settling on a pie, he picked it up carefully. He bit into the pastry and chewed slowly, his eyes closed. He popped the rest in his mouth and chewed slowly again, before swallowing. He shook his head and opened his eyes. 'I'd rather you didn't tell my mum,' he said. 'But I think it's even better than hers. And if you had ever tasted my mum's mince pies, you would know what a compliment that is.'

Freya laughed. 'I'm honoured.'

'As am I,' Callum said. 'And if the rest of the treats you make for the party are as good as this, Lady Mandeville might have you on the hook for all her parties.'

Freya laughed again. 'You'll have me blushing.'

She had expected Callum to reply with some witty comment. Instead, he smiled. It was a smile that made his eyes shine.

Sure that her cheeks were flushing, Freya pointed to her chest. 'You have some crumbs,' she said.

Callum looked down at his chest. He brushed the crumbs away from his waistcoat. 'I should let you get back to whatever it is you plan to do next, shouldn't I?' he said.

'You should,' Freya said, smiling despite herself.

'I'll stop by in a while to see how you're getting on.'

Freya nodded.

'I'll see you later, Freya.'

'I'll see you later, Callum.'

Leaving the pastry room, Callum made his way down the corridor. Freya watched him until he was out of sight. He whistled and called for Jasper. Freya listened to the latch of the door to the outside open and close. After a moment or two, she ran to the housekeeper's parlour. She looked up through the window high in the wall and watched Callum's boots in the snow, Jasper running beside him. She watched them until she couldn't see boots or paws anymore. Leaning against the radiator, she folded her arms across her chest. She waited for a moment longer, but with no further sign of Callum, she made her way back along the corridor.

In the pastry room, Freya took down the marzipan-covered cake and gave it a little tap. It had dried perfectly. She took the icing stand from the shelf, placed it on the table, and gently eased the cake from its board onto the stand.

In the mixer, she added lemon juice and egg whites to icing sugar. When the icing was the consistency she needed, she began pouring it onto the cake and smoothing it with a palette knife, working around the cake by spinning the stand. She dipped the knife in a jug of warm water from time to time, making the icing easier to work. While she worked, she let her thoughts drift back to the tour of the house. There was no doubt in her mind that she had seen the house in a period drama. It was the only way she would have known it in such detail for her brain to dredge up in her dreams. She thought back too to Callum wiping the crumbs from his chest. Each time she did, she smiled, wishing she had offered to brush them away for him.

With the cake drying in a tent of parchment paper ready for its final decoration in the morning, Freya prepared the ingredients for her gingerbread: flour, butter, sugar, treacle, ginger, nutmeg and lemon juice. The scent of spices filled the air as she beat and rolled out the mixture. She took a tin down from the shelf, opened the lid, and smiled. Each of the cutters inside held so many memories. Having them with her made it feel like Grandma was close by in this kitchen made for baking,

Choosing the cutters to use, Freya pressed the shapes into the flat mixture, making dozens of hearts and stars.

After placing the trays of gingerbread into the oven, Freya washed the cutters and put them carefully back in the tin on the shelf. When the timer sounded, she took the gingerbread from the oven and transferred them onto the cooling racks.

At just after three o'clock, Freya hung up her apron. There was time for a break before she began the final bake of the day.

In the main kitchen, she checked the windows while waiting for the kettle to boil. There was nothing to see, except a thick layer of snow. When she took her tea to the housekeeper's parlour, she looked out of those windows too. But there were no boots and no paws.

She sat in the armchair and took a sip of tea through the steam. She took another sip, and her head began to nod. She quickly shook her head to stay awake, placing her cup and saucer on the side table. She couldn't fall asleep again. But the parlour was just so warm and cosy. She focused on the tick of the clock on the mantelshelf when something nudged her leg. She looked down to find a scruffy terrier looking back at her, wagging its tail.

'Hello, Jasper,' she said. 'What are you doing here alone?'

He padded away to the door where he stopped and looked back at her.

'Are you after some food?' she asked.

Jasper tilted his head. Freya wasn't sure whether that was an answer, but she knew there was a packet of ham in the fridge in the main kitchen.

'Come on then.' She pushed down on the arms of the chair to get up. 'Let's go and see to a bit of grub.'

Freya followed Jasper out of the housekeeper's parlour. When they got to the kitchen, she stopped but Jasper carried on. 'Hey,' she called. 'What about that ham?'

Jasper paused. He looked back at her before carrying on. Freya was tempted to leave him to it. Until it occurred to her that he might have given Callum the slip. He might not even be allowed to go roaming around the posh side of the house on his own.

'Hey,' she called. 'Jasper! Come back and have a treat.' But Jasper was already halfway up the stone steps leading to the staff passageway.

'Hey,' Freya called again, following him at a jog. 'Come on, there's a good boy.' She whistled, but still it did no good. She picked up her pace but when Jasper reached the top of the steps he disappeared. Freya followed him up to the passageway and saw him trotting past the staff bells high up on the wall. She tried another whistle but if he heard it, he didn't care and disappeared through the door at the end. Freya followed him into the hallway. He seemed to be trotting but she just couldn't catch him and he was soon level with the bottom of the grand staircase. Without a care in the world, he trotted into the room at the very front of the house. Freya was pretty sure he wasn't allowed to go sniffing around and making himself comfortable on the best furniture, so she ran into the morning room after him.

The instant she crossed the threshold, Freya came to an abrupt stop. The room was familiar; there was no doubt of that. But at the same time, it felt... different. Candles glowed in the chandelier above her head and in lamps on the walls, where she was sure there had been electric bulbs. The furniture seemed different. Older. Darker. The curtains at the windows looking out over the drive were heavier, the evergreens decorating the mantelshelf more plentiful. And there was no Christmas tree.

The door opened and Freya spun around.

'Oh, hello,' a young woman said. She took a step further into the room. 'I'm sorry, I hadn't realised our guests had started to arrive.'

Freya stared at the young woman. She wore a green dress nipped in below her bust with her cleavage just visible at the square cut neckline, a little white fabric covering the swell of her breasts. Her hair was pulled back from her face with small curls sitting in front of her ears.

'You must be Mr Harris's sister,' the young woman said. 'I think you are the only guest that I am not familiar with. It is such a shame your brother cannot join us. My father was so looking forward to meeting him. But business must come first. That's what Father always says. I am glad that you were still able to join us. It's always nice to meet someone new. Please, Miss Harris,' she said, holding out her hand to a chair. 'Won't you take a seat.'

'Would you excuse me a minute?' Freya said.

'Of course,' the woman said.

Freya walked slowly to the door. For some reason, she didn't want to seem like she was out of place. That she didn't know how to behave. When in fact she couldn't have been more out of place. If there was a Christmas tree at the bottom of the stairs, then everything was fine. And something had happened which meant that the furniture in the morning room had been changed and that woman was there in preparation for the ball. That was it; she was some kind of actor who had been brought in to bring the party to life.

Freya stopped just across the threshold of the morning room.

The hallway smelled different. The air was thicker with the scent of logs burning in every fireplace. She took a step further into the hall. Flames lapped around a huge log in the grand hearth. Candles burned in sconces on the walls. There was no Christmas tree. Taking another step into the hallway, she looked to the staircase. The bannisters were still decorated with carvings of birds, animals and fruit, and still carpeted in scarlet. The floor all about her was still a mosaic of whites and bronze that sparkled in the candlelight. Candlelight! Not electric light.

Not knowing what else to do, Freya headed to the door at the back of the hallway beside the long-cased clock. Stepping through, she hurried along to the head of the stone steps leading down. Voices floated up to her. Lots of voices. She took a few steps down and saw people rushing along the basement corridor, into and out of the rooms. Maids dressed in black with crisp white aprons or darker aprons for dirtier work. A footman dressed in blue with gold braiding carried a tray of glasses from one room to another. Another carried two bottles of wine from a different room. Freya pressed against the cold stone wall. Were these people all here to help with the party too? She dipped so she could see further along the corridor. Surely they couldn't be? They couldn't have just appeared in the few minutes she had been away. Without another thought she ran down the last few steps, along the corridor and opened the door to the pastry room. A woman standing at the marble topped table looked up. When she saw Freya, she curtseyed and smiled.

'Can I help you at all, miss?' the woman asked.

Freya looked at the huge fruit cake on the table that the woman was in the process of decorating. It was at least three times the size of the cake she had prepared. And all around the cake on the table were icing decorations painted in pinks and yellows, waiting to be assembled on the cake.

Freya shook her head. 'No, thank you.'

Before the woman had a chance to say anything else, Freya ran back along the corridor, up the steps and into the staff passageway.

She emerged in the hallway and stopped. It was as she had left it moments earlier. The Candles. The smell. No Christmas tree. Below the staircase where there should have hung the portrait of Captain Thomas Mandeville on his horse, was a high console table with two cream coloured statues; one of a woman with a basket of flowers beneath her arm and the other of a man looking at her, resting on a staff.

Freya put her hand to her forehead. What was happening? This couldn't be. It just couldn't be. Callum. She needed Callum. She fumbled in her pocket for her phone. But there was no pocket. No work trousers. Instead, she wore a long, dark blue dress. She ran to the fireplace and looked in the mirror above the mantelshelf. She put her hand to her mouth and held in a noise that wanted to come out. The reflection looking back was her. She had seen that face every day for twenty-eight years. But certainty of anything else in her life vanished. The dress she wore was cinched below her bust with a low square neckline that showed off the top of her cleavage. The sleeves were long and fitted and slightly puffed at the shoulders. Her hair was pulled back tightly from her face. She could explain away everything else as some kind of miraculous and speedy transformation of Hill House in preparation for the party. It wasn't possible, but it was the only explanation that came close to making sense. What she couldn't explain was this change in her clothes. She would have known if she had slipped out of her work gear into a dress! A dress she had never seen before. And she was pretty sure she would have known if someone had styled her hair. Unless she had fallen asleep in front of the fire in the housekeeper's parlour and following Jasper up the stairs had all been a dream.

She pinched herself and instantly rubbed the area as it hurt. She looked at her reflection again, lit by the flames of the candles lining the mantelshelf. She held her hand up to a candle and pulled it away. She held it up again, moving her wrist closer to the flame and closer still. The sudden sharp pain and smell of singed hair made Freya pull her hand away. She held her wrist to her lips to try to stop the pain. It didn't stop and when she looked at her wrist, she saw a red mark already rising on the flesh.

'Miss Harris?' a voice said.

Freya turned around slowly.

The young woman smiled at her. 'Are you quite well?'

'Yes... yes,' Freya said, clutching her wrist. 'I was just a bit... a bit warm.'

'Would you like to come and sit with me awhile?' the woman asked.

Again, Freya felt like she had to go along with whatever was happening. She couldn't explain why. Other than since she had no explanation for what was happening, she would rather behave in a way that felt appropriate than add to this... this... whatever this was, by acting out of her character.

She followed the woman into the morning room.

'Please,' the woman said, holding her hand out to a chair before the fireplace, 'won't you take a seat?'

Freya sat in the chair. The pink upholstery was rich and soft. All around, exotic birds decorated the wallpaper, each one a little different than the next. There was a sheen to the walls as though it was fabric. Candles glowed amongst the waxy leaves of the holly decorating the mantelshelf.

The woman took the seat beside Freya.

'I hope I didn't upset you,' the woman said. 'Talking about your brother not being able to attend the ball.'

'No,' Freya said. 'No, you're not upsetting me.' Although why Liam was involved in this, she had no clue.

'I'm glad,' the woman said. She shook her head. 'I'm sorry,' she said. 'I don't think I have introduced myself. I'm afraid I am a little distracted today.'

Before the young woman said her name, Freya knew what it would be.

'I'm Imogen,' the young woman said. 'And I'm delighted to make your acquaintance, Miss Harris.'

'Freya,' Freya said. 'Please call me Freya.'

'What a lovely name,' Imogen said. 'Freya. I don't think I have ever heard of it before. Is it a foreign name?'

'I'm not sure,' Freya said. She wanted to pinch herself again. She was living in the dream she had created over the last few days. Living in it. Not dreaming it. She couldn't be. But she was.

'Would you care for tea?' Imogen asked.

'No, thank you,' Freya said.

Imogen smiled and smoothed down the skirt of her dress. 'I hope you don't mind that it is just me here to greet you,' she said. 'My family and the few guests who arrived yesterday have gone to spend the day with our cousins at Caxton Hall. Do you know Caxton Hall?'

'I've... um... heard of it,' Freya said. 'But I've never visited. I hear its very grand.'

Imogen laughed softly. She was as pretty as the version of the young woman in Freya's dreams. 'It is indeed very grand,' Imogen said. 'I adore my cousins, but I have to say that I find their home a little overwhelming. I prefer to spend my time at Hill House.' She leant in a little closer to Freya. 'I'm afraid I told a little untruth. I said that I had a headache so that I might stay at home. The house will be so full and so busy later preparing for the ball and then with the ball itself, that I wanted just to spend a little time alone.'

'I'm disturbing you?' Freya said.

Imogen laughed again. 'Not at all. The only reason my mother let me stay at home was because she knew you would be arriving at some point, and I could be here to greet you. I'm afraid my mother doesn't trust me to be alone currently.'

Freya knew why. Arthur Richmond. She watched Imogen look into the fire, her cheeks flushed to a warm pink. And Freya knew more than just about Arthur. She knew about Imogen's grand-mother. And her tears in the pew at the church for the loss of the woman who would have been there to help her.

Imogen shook her head. 'I'm sorry.' She turned to Freya. She smiled and it looked sweet, but Freya knew that it was painted on for her. 'Did you spend a good Christmas?' Imogen asked.

Freya knew she could say yes, that it had been nice. Quiet, but nice. That was the kind thing to say. The polite thing to say. What she had said to everyone who had asked her. And it had protected everyone around her from the truth. It had made her hide her grief that little bit more. Made her bury it a little deeper. So that it affected everyone else less but made her sadder each time. 'I spent most of it alone,' she said.

'Alone?' Imogen said. 'But your brother?'

'He has his own family.' Freya looked down to the skirt of her dress. She ran her hand over the dark fabric.

'And you did not spend it with them?' Imogen asked, her voice full of concern.

Freya shook her head. 'I wanted to spend this Christmas alone.' She looked up at Imogen who was staring at her with a slightly furrowed brow. Was she reading in Freya a kindred spirit? It was Imogen's turn to look down.

'I *felt* alone,' Imogen said. 'Even though I was surrounded by family. Going to church and then sharing a meal. And now there is all this.' She opened her arms, gesticulating widely. 'A ball for Twelfth Night. And I am to be joyful when I feel there is no joy to be found in the world.' She paused abruptly. She shook her head as though indicating she was coming to her senses. 'I must apologise, Miss Harris. Sorry, Freya. I forget myself sometimes. You do not know me. You are here at the invitation of my family to have a jolly time at the ball. Please, pay no mind to what I have just said. I get mournful sometimes. My mother has reprimanded me for it. But as I say, I am often distracted and forget the company I am in.'

In the light of the fire, Imogen seemed so young. She was a good decade younger than Freya, but the world seemed to weigh just as heavily on her shoulders.

'Do you usually enjoy the ball for Twelfth Night?' Freya asked, prompting Imogen to talk about what was troubling her. If she wanted to.

Imogen smiled. 'Very much. Very much indeed. Everyone we know in the county is invited. There is dancing and music and games and the food. Oh, the food! All of our relatives and the friends of our acquaintance would tell you it is the best evening of the year. The very best party. And there is so much fun to be had. But this year…' Her words trailed away, and her smile disappeared.

'This year?' Freya said, leaving her words as a question.

Imogen continued to look into the flames in the hearth. 'This year, the person who made it the best party will not be there. And there will be someone there who is the other good person I know, and I must have nothing to do with him.'

To anyone else, Imogen's words may have made no sense. But they made perfect sense to Freya. And the pain in the eyes of this young girl – the tears that sat, waiting to be spilled – held a mirror up to her own pain. Her own sadness. Her own loss. And this moment was real. So very real. Whatever may happen after it, she didn't know, but for now, this was her reality, and she couldn't bear to see the pain of that girl and do nothing about it.

'I lost my grandmother this year too,' Freya said softly.

Imogen looked up. She stared at Freya for a few moments. 'I'm so sorry,' she said.

Freya felt her bottom lip start to tremble. 'It's difficult, isn't it?' she said.

Imogen nodded again. Freya could only imagine that her expression was the same as Imogen's.

'My grandmother was my best friend,' Freya said.

'As was mine.' Imogen looked into the flames again. 'I have a twin – Rebecca. She is the kindest and sweetest girl you could ever hope to meet. We have always been encouraged to be best friends. My mother encouraged us to be each other's confidantes and preferred us not to have close friendships with girls outside the house. I love Rebecca dearly and would give my life to save hers, but she is different to me. It would not be fair to unburden to her and to test where her loyalties within our family lie. She is an obedient daughter to my parents. Whereas I… My grandmother understood me. Is that how you felt about your grandmother?'

It felt to Freya as though they were dancing around each other, testing how much they should say. She wanted to be honest. 'My parents died in an accident when I was small. My grandparents brought me up.'

'I'm so sorry,' Imogen said. 'I shouldn't say these things about my family, they are unfair.'

'You should say how you feel,' Freya said. She paused. She stared at the dark blue skirt of her dress. 'There's something I haven't told anyone,' she said. 'That I haven't wanted to admit even to myself.'

She felt Imogen watching her. She could stop this now. She could swallow down the words that she hadn't wanted to even think but that had forced their way to the surface so often recently. 'I'm jealous,' she said quietly. 'Of my brother. Of his happiness.' The bark of a log crackled in the fire. 'I spent ten years taking care of my grandmother after my grandfather died. I wouldn't have had it any other way. I wouldn't have missed a single minute that I had with her. But... My brother will use his inheritance to improve his home. He has a wife and children with another child on the way. His inheritance will bring him happiness. I will use my inheritance to buy a small property. But the thought of it brings me no joy. I will be leaving the only home I can remember to live alone. I will be leaving all my memories. My inheritance will bring me only sadness.' A tear slipped down Freya's cheek. She tried to wipe it away, but her hands wouldn't move. Imogen had leant forward and was holding Freya's hands in hers.

'I am so very sorry,' Imogen said. 'And I don't think you are jealous of your brother's happiness. Rather, you are sad for your own situation. Anyone would be in your position.' Her hands were so soft and so warm and as reassuring as her words.

Freya nodded slowly. 'You're right,' she said. 'I love my brother and his family. I want nothing but the best for them. I just feel so lost. I'm sorry,' she said. 'I shouldn't be unburdening my problems on you.'

She felt her hands squeezed. 'My grandmother taught me that everyone needs a confidante,' Imogen said. 'I could talk to her about everything. And I like to think I can fulfil that role for anyone who needs me.'

Freya looked up to find Imogen looking back at her with so much kindness. She was still holding Freya's hands.

'Tell me more about your grandmother,' Freya said. 'I'd like to hear about her.'

A smile lit Imogen's face. 'Are you sure?' she said.

Freya nodded.

Imogen gave Freya's hands another squeeze. 'My grandmother made me feel that I could achieve anything with my life,' Imogen said. 'And I believed it. With her here, I knew she would have supported me in anything I wanted to do. I have always wanted to use my position to help other people. Not in a way where I would sit around with other rich women and their daughters and raise a bit of charitable money. But real work. Hard work that would help other people. But without her here these are all just fantasies. My mother will not allow me to do anything. In her mind the greatest thing she can do is have me presented to the queen next year so that I will be out on the market for eligible bachelors to pore over. And once she has me shackled to one of them, that will be her job done. She can wash her hands of me and leave me to my husband.'

'Do you really think that's all your mother wants for you?' Freya asked.

Imogen sighed. She let her hands fall from Freya's. 'I'm being unkind. I know my mother thinks it's what's best for me. But surely, I should be allowed to decide that myself. My mother thinks differently to me. I want to live a good and a productive life. Not just decorate the arm of a man and arrange parties and host teas. I want to contribute to society and chose my own path in life. My brother is allowed to, why not me?'

'Can't you try to tell her?'

'She will not listen to me. Had my grandmother still been here, she would have pled my case. No, she would not have pled it. She would have told my mother what needed to happen. She was my father's mother so had been the wife of my grandfather – the previous baronet. And my mother was in awe of her. And a little afraid. She would take counsel from her in a way that she will not listen to me.'

'Can your father not help?' Freya asked.

Imogen laughed sadly. 'He leaves all things to do with my sister and me with my mother. If anything, I think he would like to see us wedded even quicker than my mother would. He would then be rid of the financial responsibility of us.' She paused. Shook her head. 'I am being so unkind. And my parents don't deserve it. I find that since my grandmother passed I am angry all the time. Even when I might be a little happy, there is this constant fury that sits just below the surface waiting to come out. Is that how you feel?'

Freya paused before nodding. 'I'm angry that my home has to be sold. I'm angry that my grandmother has gone and that I feel so alone.'

'And are you angry that everyone else has been able to go on with their lives and you are stuck in your sadness?'

'I am,' Freya said. She felt a tear slip down her cheek and watched Imogen wipe away her own tear.

'And do you feel that your grandmother is sometimes with you when it is impossible?' Imogen said. 'As though she is still trying to guide you in life and help you.'

'I do,' Freya said, 'I really do. It doesn't seem possible that she's not somewhere.'

'That's how I feel,' Imogen said. 'So much life can surely not simply disappear.' She laughed a little sadly. 'I'm afraid that it would seem we have much in common.' Her damp eyes glistened in the firelight. 'Perhaps if you lived closer, we might be friends. I know I am much younger than you and you might find me a little silly, but I feel you understand me. Perhaps we would make each other less angry.'

Freya leant forward. It was her turn to take Imogen's hands in hers. 'For a start, I don't think you're silly. And the difference in our ages wouldn't mean anything to me in terms of being your friend. But I will be going far away soon.' She thought carefully about how to frame her next words. 'Isn't there anybody else you are close to?'

Imogen seemed to think for a moment again. 'Do you know the Richmonds?'

'I know of them,' Freya said.

'Their son, Arthur. He understands me.' Imogen glanced at the door. She lowered her voice. 'We have known each other since we were small children. But recently... I care for him more than I dare to say. But my mother will not have it.' She glanced at the door again. 'Do you have someone you care for in that way, Freya?'

Freya felt Imogen squeeze her hands. She could say there was no one. And just yesterday that would have been true. 'There is someone,' she said. 'But I hardly know him. I'm sure he doesn't—'

'Does he make your heart sing?' Imogen's voice was little more than a whisper when she leant in closer. 'Does he occupy your every waking moment?'

'He's starting to,' Freya said.

'What's his name?' Imogen said.

'Callum,' Freya said. 'His name is Callum.'

A sudden call from the hall made Imogen jump to her feet.

The door flew open. A young woman rushed into the room. She still wore a bonnet, and her short jacket had snow on the shoulders. Freya recognised her instantly.

'Imogen,' Rebecca said. 'Mother wants...' She stopped when she saw Freya.

'Oh, I'm so sorry,' Rebecca said. 'I didn't realise our company had arrived.'

Freya got to her feet.

'This is Miss Harris. Miss Freya Harris,' Imogen said. 'She is the sister of Mr Harris who Father invited to the party. We are lucky that she still came even though her brother had to return to town on business. Miss Harris, this is my sister, Rebecca.'

'Miss Harris,' Rebecca said, crossing the room. 'How delightful it is to meet you. I am so sorry to have barged in like that.'

'It's all right,' Freya said. 'I don't mind.'

Rebecca turned to her sister. 'I ran ahead. Mother wants to see you the instant she gets home. I don't know why, but it will be in just a few moments. You should come with me. Would you excuse us, Miss Harris?'

'Of course,' Freya said.

Rebecca left the room, but Imogen didn't follow instantly. Instead, she turned to Freya. 'Thank you,' she said. 'For letting me talk about my grandmother. It feels as though nobody wants to talk of her anymore. And it was all trapped inside me. Like pain without a cure. I know you understand what I mean. Perhaps we can talk later, at the ball. I should so like to tell you about Arthur Richmond and seek your advice. And to hear all about your Callum.'

'All right,' Freya said. Even as she said the words, she had no idea if she would still be there for the ball.

'Until this evening, Freya,' Imogen said. She ran to the door, turning back only briefly to smile at her.

Freya stood for a moment looking at the place where Imogen had stood. She looked around the room at the delicate birds painted onto the wallpaper, the finely upholstered furniture, the red berries nestled amongst the dark green holly on the mantelshelf. The scent of woodsmoke filled the room. As it had when she woke from her dreams of Imogen. But this wasn't a dream.

Freya walked to the door and stepped through. A Christmas tree stood beside the hearth in the hallway. The air was still and calm. There was the scent of pine from the Christmas tree. Glass baubles swayed slightly on its branches. There was just the faintest smell of woodsmoke from the single log in the hearth beside the tree.

Freya ran to the mirror. Gone was the blue dress, replaced by her work t-shirt and trousers. A sound came from the direction of the morning room and in the mirror, she saw Jasper tip-tapping his way across the hall. He stopped at her feet, and she stooped to scoop him into her arms. His fur was soft and warm. He was real. Very real. And he didn't seem to mind being held.

'What just happened, Jasper?' she whispered to the dog, holding him tight. 'Was I dreaming. I can't have been. But... Were you in the room all that time? Did you see her too?'

Jasper's answer was to lick Freya's cheek. She held him closer still. What had she been expecting? That a dog would turn around and give her some answers?

Still holding Jasper, she made her way to the back of the hall, past Captain Thomas Mandeville who had been reinstated to his place on the wall below the stairs. The staff passageway was empty, as was the basement corridor – no maids or footmen. She passed the pastry room – no pastry cook, just the scent of cinnamon, nutmeg and marzipan. Still with Jasper in her arms, she returned to the housekeeper's parlour. She paced up and down in the room, from the hearth to the small dining table and back again. The silver lametta on the branches of the Christmas tree twisted and danced in the breeze she created. The paperchains swayed gently above her head.

'It can't be real,' Freya said, and kissed Jasper on the top of his head. There was something reassuring about holding the living, breathing dog in her arms. He was warm and alive and real. But Imogen had felt real and alive too. They had held hands and Imogen's hands were warm and soft. And there had been something so cathartic in speaking to someone who had been through the same experience, who felt the way she did, especially someone as lovely as Imogen. Was it possible to wish a thing into existence just because you needed it? Freya shook her head and continued to pace. They had agreed to meet that night so Imogen could speak to her about Arthur. She couldn't just snap her fingers and go back in time. She would let Imogen down. But how could she let someone down who was probably a figment of her imagination. Scratch that. Was definitely a figment of her imagination. Because how could any of this be real?

Freya sat down heavily in the chair and put Jasper down on the floor. He stayed close to her legs. What was very real was what she had said to Imogen. About how she had recently felt towards Liam. And Imogen had been right. It wasn't resentment. Liam was her brother. She loved him and his family very much. Her feelings had been muddled, what with the sale of the house and all that still had to be done. What she had thought was jealousy towards Liam was in fact sadness at her own situation. Imogen was so perceptive for someone so young. She had an aura of kindness. Perhaps that's why she had confided in her about Callum. Freya covered her eyes with her hand. Callum. Was he occupying her every waking moment? Did he make her heart sing? As she had said to Imogen, he was starting to. But she still knew nothing about him. If he was married or involved or engaged.

Freya jumped from the chair. 'This isn't getting me anywhere,' she said to Jasper, who still sat at her feet. 'And those biscuits aren't going to make themselves.' Even so, she couldn't help glancing over her shoulder to the window high in the wall, looking for boots in the snow.

Jasper led the way out of the housekeeper's parlour and dipped into the main kitchen. Freya followed him. 'Did you want that ham now?' she asked. Jasper stood at an empty bowl, one paw raised. Freya took the packet from the fridge and tipped the slices into the bowl. Jasper ate speedily and licked the bowl clean before retreating to a dog bed tucked into the corner of the room.

Freya dropped the empty packet in the bin, took her phone from her pocket and typed out a message.

> Jasper in the kitchen. Just in case you were missing him. Gave him ham.

Before pressing send, she double checked that she hadn't added any kisses.

In the pastry room, Freya closed the door. She took her headphones from her bag and put them on before selecting some music from her phone. She picked a best of ABBA and lined up a Kylie Minogue playlist to follow. At the sink, she began to scrub her hands. But as the hot water hit, she pulled away. A blister had bubbled on her wrist. She ran the cold tap and held her wrist beneath the freezing water. Burns were an occupational hazard for a baker. But this blister hadn't been caused by accidentally touching the element in an oven.

This blister covered the burn from where she had held her hand to the flame of the candle on the mantelshelf in the hallway.

ELEVEN

By the time the playlist came to an end, Freya had two batches of Shrewsbury cakes and two batches of Rout cakes cooling. Every inch of wire rack was covered in cakes. The Shrewsbury cakes weren't really cakes at all, but heavily spiced biscuits that she had cut out into the shapes of stars. The Rout cakes were cakes of a kind. Again, heavily spiced and with plenty of dried fruit and a good glug of sherry. As they cooked, they spread to form a thin sort of cake.

Freya lifted the parchment paper from the Twelfth Night cake and gave it a tap with her knuckle. The icing was setting nicely and would be ready to decorate in the morning. She looked down her list. With the Shrewsbury and Rout cakes made, there really was just the Twelfth Night cake to decorate and the marzipan cake to make. She tapped her pen to her cheek. She had enough ingredients to make another batch of each cake. And she really was ahead of where she needed to be for the day. She glanced at her watch. It was just after six o'clock. The washing up was all done. Perhaps she should treat herself to a cup of tea before deciding how to spend the rest of the evening. Maybe another batch of gingerbread would go down well.

After tidying the table and counter tops, Freya pulled her

apron over her head and hung it on the hook. She took off her head-phones and put them in her bag before tucking her folder beneath her arm.

She was just one step outside the pastry room when she heard noises from the main kitchen. She stopped. She looked down at the blister on her wrist. Whatever fantasy her mind had cooked up for her earlier couldn't be happening again. Because that's what it had been. An hallucination. She must have been tired after working in the morning. And somehow her mind had played a trick on her. Or she'd had another of her vivid dreams. She had been sleepy before Jasper found her and she followed him up to the morning room. Perhaps that had been a dream too and reality only started when she got up to feed him ham.

Freya marched towards the kitchen. She walked through the open door and stopped. Callum looked up from the table. He was wearing an apron over his shirt; his jacket and waistcoat were draped over the back of a chair. He was in the process of rolling out pastry while a warming meat smell came from a pan on the range. The kitchen was in chaos with bowls and chopping boards and utensils and packets spread across the table and on the draining board. Callum's hands were covered in flour, and he pushed his fringe back from his face with his wrist. 'Steak pie do you?' he asked.

'I beg your pardon?' Freya said.

'For dinner. Steak pie with mash and veg. It's not fancy, but I'm told it's quite tasty and it's very wholesome on a cold winter's night.'

'I didn't even think about dinner,' Freya said. 'I could have ordered something.'

Callum glanced up to the windows and to the snow still falling against the black backdrop of night. 'If we can't get out, they can't get in.'

'Pardon?'

'There's no way a driver could get up the lane to deliver food.

I'm afraid we are cut off from the outside world until the big thaw comes overnight.'

Freya hadn't forgotten about Callum's offer for her to stay. But she had been too busy to give it too much thought. 'I don't want to be any trouble...' she said.

'It's no trouble. You have to eat. I have to eat. And you have been busy all afternoon. The smells coming from the pastry room have had my mouth watering.'

'Rosewater,' Freya said. 'And orange essence. And nutmeg and cinnamon.'

'The Mandevilles and their guests are in for a real treat tomorrow,' Callum said. He looked up at her. When he smiled, she remembered what she had said to Imogen. Even if it had been a dream, she had said. it. She was glad that Callum looked down and wouldn't see her cheeks flush.

Taking up the rolling pin, Callum grabbed another handful of flour from a packet and scattered it across the table. 'What have you got there?' he asked, nodding to the file under Freya's arm as he began rolling again.

'It's my notes,' she said. 'And recipes.'

'Why not pop it down on the side there,' Callum said. 'Red or white?'

'Excuse me?' Freya said, placing her file on the countertop closest to the door.

'Wine. Red or white.'

'I don't think I should drink. I can get on with more work tonight.'

Callum put the rolling pin down. 'Tonight? I would say you've done a full day's work already, haven't you?'

'I could do more.'

'Is there more on your schedule for today?'

'No. But there's always more that can be done.'

Callum took up his rolling pin and began rolling out the pastry again. 'It's completely up to you,' he said. 'Dinner will be another hour or so.'

Freya looked at Callum working in his apron, his hands covered in flour, his hair falling forward. She would rather stay with him. *Much* rather. Which probably meant she shouldn't.

'I'll stay,' she said, before she could stop herself. 'But only if I can help.'

Callum smiled. 'I'm glad. He's useless company.' He nodded to Jasper, fast asleep in his basket in the corner. 'He'll only budge if there's the sign of a treat in it for him. Isn't that right boy!'

Jasper lifted his ear before tucking further into a nose-to-tail ball.

'Thanks for looking after him this afternoon,' Callum said. 'He has a habit of wandering off, especially if he thinks there's the chance of charming a visitor into a spot of food.'

Freya thought back to the afternoon. To following Jasper up the stairs. To imagining Imogen in the morning room. Or dreaming her. 'I hope it was okay,' she said quickly. 'Giving him some ham.'

'Oh, he's a dustbin,' Callum said. 'Any scrap will find a grateful home in that cast iron stomach of his.'

Freya looked over the chaos on the table. 'What can I do?' she asked.

'Spuds,' Callum said. 'In the sink. They want peeling. And will carrots and peas do you?'

'They will,' Freya said.

Callum was looking down at the pastry so didn't see her smile at him. She grabbed a spare apron from a hook on the wall and pulled it on. She stood at the sink, ran the water and began peeling the pile of potatoes, adding them to a colander already waiting. She wanted to turn and look over her shoulder but settled on watching the snow falling outside so that it sat deep on the gravel at ground level.

'It's thick out there, isn't it?' Callum said.

Had he been watching her? No, wishful thinking. 'Do you really think it will melt by the morning?' Freya asked.

'We have a bit of a microclimate here,' Callum said. 'The weather can be different to the weather just a few miles down the road. But I'm sure it will melt. If not, I'll be busy with the truck and salting the approach lane in the morning.'

Freya smiled as she began to peel a carrot. Callum had a lovely, dry sense of humour to along with the looks. *Stop it*, she said to herself. And to Callum, said, 'Shall I chop these up?'

'Please,' Callum said. 'The chopping board's in the cupboard under the sink and you can find a knife in the drawer of the dresser.'

Sinking to her haunches, Freya found the chopping board. She turned to the dresser. Callum was in the process of transferring the meat into a pie dish. Steam filled the air around him.

'That smell's delicious,' she said, watching him spread out the meaty gravy.

'It's my speciality,' Callum said. 'Actually,' he said, placing the pan back on the range. 'It was this or a roast chicken. Spaghetti at a push.'

'I would have been happy with any of those,' Freya said. 'I've been living on microwave meals for months.'

'Oh?' Callum said. 'I thought as a baker it would be all home cooked and fresh.'

It was an innocent enough comment and he didn't seem to be fishing for an explanation. 'I've been busy,' Freya said.

'Makes sense,' Callum said. 'With Christmas. I bet that keeps anyone in your line of work on their toes!'

Freya forced a smile and took a knife from the drawer. She returned to the sink without looking back at Callum. It hadn't been a lie, but it felt off not to tell him the truth. Chopping up the potatoes, she pushed them from the board into a pan. And then she prepared the carrots.

'All done?' Callum asked.

'All done,' Freya said. 'I should go to check on the last bake.'

'There's plenty of time,' Callum said. 'I still have to get this pie in the oven.'

. . .

Back in the pastry room, Freya transferred the cooled bakes into tins. She washed up the wire racks and placed them on the draining board. It felt wrong not to be honest with Callum. He was being so kind in cooking her a meal. He probably wouldn't mind that she hadn't been completely honest. She was just someone he had brought in to work for a few days. But still, it didn't sit right.

After spending longer than was really necessary wiping down the surfaces and cleaning the floor in preparation for the next day, Freya turned out the light. Closing the door behind her, she was met with the sound of music coming from the kitchen. And singing. A deep baritone singing along softly to what sounded like opera. Freya stood just beyond the door and listened. Callum was a good singer. A very good singer.

When the song ended and another started, Freya stepped from behind the door and into the kitchen.

'Finished for the day?' Callum asked. The chaos from earlier was gone. The flour and ingredients and utensils all cleared away and the kitchen spotless. Callum was setting plates down at the end of the table that had been laid with a white tablecloth, cutlery and glasses. The main lights were out, and the kitchen was lit by the fairy lights strung across the chimneybreast and candles lined up on the table. Soothing cello music floated from the old-fashioned radio on the dresser.

'You shouldn't have gone to all this trouble,' Freya said.

'Do you think I don't have linen, fine china and candles every evening?' Callum asked.

'Sorry,' Freya said.

Callum laughed. 'I'm joking. It's usually something on toast on a tray while I watch a bit of telly. I thought as it's one of the only times this year I'm likely to cook, I should serve it properly.'

'I'm very grateful,' Freya said.

'You haven't tasted it yet,' Callum laughed.

Freya watched him adjust a napkin.

'Can I say something?' she said.

'Of course.' Callum turned the dial on the radio and the music stopped. He rested against the dresser, arms folded across his broad chest. The apron was gone, and he wore just his shirt tucked into his jeans with his waistcoat over his shirt.

Freya could see his muscles press against his sleeves. She pictured him slipping the tweed waistcoat back on after removing the apron, fastening the buttons, the dark hair at the base of each finger. She swallowed.

'Earlier today,' she said, 'you thought I was distracted. And just before, you asked why I was eating microwave meals.' She paused and took a breath. 'I hate to lie. Or not explain myself properly. You see... my grandmother... she died last summer. We ran the bakery business together. And I've been finding it hard. Very hard. We lived together as well. She... my parents died when I was very small, and my grandma and grandad took me and my brother in. They brought us up. I got a message this morning to say the house is on the market. It has to be sold. And I have to find somewhere else to buy. That's why I wasn't quite myself this afternoon. This is my first job since she died. When you phoned, I had nothing else to do. I spent Christmas alone.' The more she spoke, the more she felt she wanted to say or that she had to say to explain herself. 'I tried a New Year's party, but it didn't work out. And I just wanted to explain that, so I wasn't being untruthful.'

Callum made his way around the table. He stopped just before reaching her. 'I'm so sorry, Freya,' he said softly.

'Everyone's been very kind,' she said. 'And my friends are so good.'

'But they're not there when you close the door every night,' Callum said.

Freya looked up at Callum. 'How did you know?'

He smiled sadly. 'My father died a few years ago. I saw what my mother had to go through. When you're used to living with someone you love for so many years, and then they're not there anymore, the house is empty.'

'I'm sorry you lost your father,' Freya said.

'It was a while ago now,' he said. 'But I remember how it feels.

Your grandparents must have been a wonderful people to take in two small children. Did your grandmother teach you to bake?'

Freya nodded.

'She did a fine job,' Callum said. 'Of teaching you and raising you.'

All Freya could do was look at the front of Callum's shirt. When she found her voice, she said, 'Thank you.'

'So,' Callum said, his voice lightening. 'Red or white?'

Freya looked up into his face. He was smiling at her. She laughed. 'Red, please.'

'Merlot?'

'Perfect.'

Callum took a bottle from the counter. He removed the cork and poured two glasses. Handing one to Freya, he held up his own glass. 'What shall we toast?'

'To a successful party tomorrow,' Freya said.

'To a successful party tomorrow,' Callum repeated, and chinked his glass to Freya's. She took a sip.

'Okay?' Callum asked.

'Okay,' Freya said.

'Take a seat,' Callum said. 'I'll be serving up in a few minutes.'

He held out a chair and Freya sat down. She took another sip of wine. 'It smells really good,' she said.

'The proof of the pudding!' Callum said, and busied himself at the range. Freya watched him. He had known exactly the right words to say. He hadn't lingered on her sadness, which always made it worse somehow. He had shared his experiences, said such kind things about her grandparents, and punctured her melancholy with his humour.

'Are you sure I can't help?' she asked.

Callum took a teaspoon of mashed potato from the pan. 'You can tell me if this needs more butter. Or salt.'

He handed the spoon to Freya. She blew on it. Tasting the mash, she closed her eyes. 'Perfect,' she said.

Callum took the spoon from her and placed it in the sink. With his back to Freya, he looked over the pans. The paperchains above him swayed in the warm air from the range. The flames of the candles lined up on the table danced. Freya took another sip of wine.

Putting on a pair of oven gloves, Callum took the pie from the oven and placed it on a mat on the table. 'I know I'm in the presence of a pastry expert,' he said. 'But I hope this isn't disappointing.'

'So far, so good,' Freya said, looking over the golden-brown crust. 'Great crimping skills.'

Callum laughed. 'High praise indeed,' he said. He served the food and sat down opposite Freya. He placed his napkin in his lap. 'Tuck in,' he said.

Freya placed her napkin in her lap and took up her cutlery. The hot, richly scented steam was delicious in itself but when Freya tasted the pie, she had to close her eyes again. 'This is really good,' she said.

'I'm glad you like it,' Callum said. He chewed a mouthful of pie and picked up his glass. He held it Freya. 'To sharing a homecooked meal,' he said.

'To sharing a homecooked meal,' Freya repeated, taking a sip of wine to mask her smile.

TWELVE

After finishing their meal, Freya stood beside Callum while he washed up. She dried each item and placed everything on the table to be put away.

Callum craned to look up through the window. 'It's still coming down,' he said. He looked over his shoulder to Jasper who was enjoying his share of the pie. 'No going out for you tonight, I'm afraid,' he said to the dog. But Jasper was too busy with his nose in his bowl to take any notice.

After washing the final pan, Callum dried his hands. 'I'm sorry there's no dessert,' he said. 'There's cheese and crackers we could have later if you're peckish.'

Freya picked up a wooden spoon and wiped it with the tea towel. 'Thank you,' she said. 'For dinner. And for all this.'

'It's the least I could do,' Callum said. 'You've put in a lot of effort today.'

'It's what I'm paid for.'

'You went over and above,' Callum said. 'And I think you know it.' He rolled the sleeves of his shirt down.

Freya watched him. The muscles contracting in his arms, the fine hairs covering his skin, his fingers fastening the buttons at his cuffs. She felt her cheeks warm. She went to place the spoon on the table but put it too close to the edge. It tipped and clattered to the floor. She knelt to collect it but didn't realise that Callum had done the same thing until she made to pick up the spoon and put her hand over his. She pulled her hand away.

'I'm so sorry,' she said.

They stayed there for a moment. Callum still held the spoon. Freya looked at Callum. His eyes seemed to smile. She had to stop herself putting her hand over his again. He stood up and Freya followed. He placed the spoon on the table and picked up the bottle of wine.

'Shall we finish this?' he asked.

'It would be rude not to,' Freya surprised herself by saying. The Merlot had clearly loosened her mood. And her tongue. And her ability to dry up without incident.

Callum held out the chair for Freya to sit again. He pinched the knees of his dark jeans and sat in his chair. He took a sip of his wine. The soft light from the candles picked out his features.

'I feel very underdressed,' Freya said, glancing down at her beige trousers and white t-shirt, hoping Callum heard the joke in her voice and forgot about the spoon mishap. 'Me in my work clothes and you in your tweed waistcoat.' She picked up her glass and took a sip of wine.

'That's your uniform,' Callum said. 'This is mine. If you'd grown up where I did, you'd see everyone working in the old houses or on the big country estates dresses as I do. It's for convenience. And warmth. It gets mighty chilly way up north! Which is why I favour tweeds over a kilt. It can get a bit blustery.'

Freya nearly choked on her mouthful of wine.

Callum laughed out loud, a deep baritone of a laugh. 'Would you like me to pat you on the back?' he asked.

Freya shook her head as she swallowed the wine through her laugh.

'Sorry,' Callum said, still laughing that deep laugh. 'I forget myself sometimes. My sense of humour can be a bit raw for some.'

'It's not that,' Freya said. 'You just caught me off guard. I like a dry sense of humour.'

'Good,' Callum said. 'I'm glad.' He picked up his glass and held it aloft for a second to Freya before taking a sip.

'I hope you won't take this the wrong way,' Freya said. 'But when I first met you, I thought you were a bit old-fashioned. I think it's the tweeds and the Scottish accent. It's so gentle.'

It was Callum's turn to almost choke on his mouthful of wine. 'Gentle?' He laughed. 'Ach, I suppose I may have a touch of Mrs Doubtfire about me.' He put on a fake very soft Scottish accent which made Freya laugh again. 'But don't let it fool you,' Callum said. 'Most of my extended family are from Glasgow!' He changed his accent. It was harder and far more powerfully Scottish. Returning to his normal accent, he said, 'My direct line moved just north of Glasgow a few generations back. My three times great-grandparents met working on the Candallan estate owned by the family of a woman who married into the Mandevilles. She was the great-great-grandmother of the current baronet. Over the years the staff of Hill House and the Candallan estate have been a bit inter-changeable. My mother still works on the estate, and my brother manages it. I made my way down here when the Mandevilles were looking for a new estate manager for Hill House.'

'It must be a lot of work,' Freya said.

'It is,' Callum said. 'But it keeps me out of trouble. I know it has the motorway running at the end of the drive and a great deal of the land was sold off for the council's housing estate. But there's still a good-sized estate to manage with the woodland, parkland and farms off towards the west. And there's still the lake just beyond the woods.' He took a sip of wine and sat further back in his seat.

'So, you're happy here?' Freya asked.

'Very,' Callum said. 'There's something special about this place. Nobody visits just once. This house and land, it gets into your blood.' He paused. He placed his hand on the table and moved it backwards and forwards.

'What is it?' Freya asked.

Callum looked at her. Really looked at her. He ran his fingers through his hair. 'You've been very honest with me,' he said. 'About your grandmother. That can't be easy to talk about.' He paused again.

Freya shook her head. 'It isn't.'

'But you felt comfortable enough to confide in me?' Callum's voice was soft and low. And it seemed he was posing a question.

'I did.' Freya smiled. She hoped it was reassuring.

'I *am* happy here,' Callum said. 'But I miss this.'

Freya waited for him to elaborate. When he didn't, she said, 'This?'

'A proper conversation. I talk to people all day. Everyone here at Hill House is great. A real team. But I miss having deeper conversations.'

'Oh,' Freya said, hoping her cheeks weren't flushing from the wine.

'When I lived at home,' Callum said. 'We used to all get around the table for dinner to share what our days had been like. Me, my mum, my brother and his wife and my two younger sisters when they were home from university. I don't regret coming to Hill House. I had to stretch my wings. I was always in my brother's shadow. He was the oldest and ran the estate at Candallan. I worked for him. And it was right that I follow my own path. But I miss my family.' He laughed under his breath. 'I really miss having meaningful conversations where there's a connection.' He pushed his hair away from his face. 'There, I haven't told anyone that. Not even my mum.'

Freya twisted her glass on the table. 'Thank you,' she said. 'For sharing that with me.'

'Thank you for this evening,' Callum said. 'And for the conversation.'

Freya couldn't help but smile. She couldn't hide it. 'It's been my best evening this festive season,' she said. 'I haven't felt at all

Christmassy...' she looked up at the paperchains and to the string of fairy lights and the candles glowing softly '...until now.'

Callum sat back in his chair. 'I'm glad,' he said. 'It's fast becoming my best evening too.' He took a sip of his wine. 'It's nice to have such good company.'

Freya tried to hide yet another smile. Was she reading too much into this situation? Probably. 'Are you often on your own here?' she asked.

'Occasionally,' Callum said. 'And it can be very quiet when the Mandevilles and the other staff are away. But I never feel alone. I can walk around this house and just feel that it is alive around me.' He laughed under his breath and shook his head. 'I know that sounds a bit mad. Like I'm going stir crazy in the big old house. It's not that at all. It just feels so warm and full of life.'

Freya sat forward. 'I don't think that sounds crazy. Actually, today—'

Before she could continue, Jasper jumped suddenly into Callum's lap. 'Whoa there boy,' Callum said. 'What's got into you! He doesn't usually do that,' he said to Freya. 'Jasper isn't much of a lapdog. Is it more treats you want?' he said, stroking the dog's head. 'Come on then.'

Putting Jasper on the floor, Callum scooped a little more of the meat from the pie and put it into the bowl on the floor.

Freya drained her glass. Had she really been about to tell Callum about what had happened today. Upstairs. In the morning room? Just because he said the house felt alive, he wouldn't have meant that literally. Thank heavens for Jasper's stomach. Without it, she could have said anything...

'Fancy a coffee?' Callum asked, taking a pot down from the dresser.

'Please,' Freya said.

'Why don't you go through to the housekeeper's parlour,' Callum said. 'I laid a fire in there earlier so it should be good and warm by now.'

Freya collected her file from the dresser and made her way

through to the parlour. She sat in one of the two armchairs before the fireplace. Putting her file down on the side table, she held her palms out to the flames. A coffee was what she needed to dilute the Merlot. And to stop her saying things she would regret.

'Here we are,' Callum said, pushing the door open with his foot. He placed a tray down on the small dining table, the coffee pot steaming. 'Milk and sugar?' he asked.

'Milk and one sugar, please,' Freya said.

Callum stirred the coffee and handed a cup and saucer to Freya.

He sat in the armchair on the other side of the fireplace. 'I was thinking,' he said. 'About what you said earlier. You'll be looking to buy somewhere soon. Would it be local to here?'

Freya took a sip of her hot coffee and nodded.

'Do you have anyone who can take a look at properties for you?' Callum asked. He took a sip of his coffee. 'Someone that knows them. You can tell me to mind my own business. For all I know you're a dab hand at DIY and property maintenance.'

'I'm not,' Freya said.

'If you needed someone, I'd be happy to take a look for you. I've spent my whole life working on houses, so I know a thing or two about what to look for.'

'You'd do that for me?' Freya said. 'But... you don't know me.'

'I was brought up to help people if they need it. It would be what, an hour or so out of my day each time? I'm no surveyor but I could look for anything obvious that might ring alarm bells.' He took another sip of coffee. 'You've got my number. Just phone me when you need to.'

It was all Freya could do not to cry. People had been kind to her over the months. But this was different. A person she had known for just one day was prepared to help her. Callum had cooked her a meal and made her feel so very welcome when he knew nothing about her. 'Thank you,' she said. It was all she could say.

Callum smiled. 'That fire's taken well,' he said.

Freya looked into the flames and nodded.

'More coffee?' Callum asked.

'Thank you,' Freya said.

Callum collected the coffee pot from the table and as he did so, an ice-cold breeze rushed into the room.

Callum placed the coffee pot back on the tray. Getting up from the armchair, Freya followed him out into the corridor. The door to the outside stood open.

'Dammit,' Callum said. 'I knew I should have fixed that dodgy lock. The wind must have caught it.'

He had to give it a good shove to close the door. He turned the key in the lock and as he was about to bolt the top, Freya saw the distinct shape of a dog at the top of the steps outside. It was only there for a second before disappearing into the dark night.

'Jasper!' she said, pointing to the top of the steps. 'He was there.'

'Oh, crap!' Callum said. He fumbled to turn the key in the lock, yanked the door open with force and was outside almost before Freya knew what was happening. 'Jasper!' he called 'Jasper! Good boy. Come here.'

Callum took the steps up to ground level two at a time and disappeared into the darkness. Freya stood in the doorway. The snow came down heavily and it landed on the mat inside. She shivered and put her arms around herself. Should she run out to help look for Jasper or was it best for her to stay inside? She took a few steps up and looked through the snow to the dark Hill House land. She could hear Callum faintly in the distance calling out. He must be freezing out there without a coat on. Freya took the final steps up so that she was standing on the path behind the house. Or where the path should have been. The snow was thick. So thick. She walked in the direction of Callum's calls, the snow up to her shins, soaking her trainers and trousers. Fat flakes landed on her eyelids and in her hair. Callum's voice disappeared. The snow squeaked beneath the soles of her trainers. It was so dark that all she could see was snow swirling against the black sky and the outline of trees. Perhaps Jasper was hiding. Perhaps he hadn't actually ventured far from the house. 'Jasper?' Freya called. 'Jasper! Where are you boy?' She took a few more steps, wading through the snow. She became aware of the sound of someone else moving through the snow. She stopped. She wiped her eyes and looked around. The sound continued even though she wasn't moving. The only tracks in the snow were hers. It wasn't possible that someone was walking towards her without leaving tracks.

'Callum, is that you?' she said. No response. She began walking backwards, towards the house. When she felt a presence behind her, she stopped and spun around, nearly falling over. There was no one there. Still the snow fell heavily. She wiped her eyes again but still had the feeling that someone was standing at her shoulder. She stood absolutely still.

'The woodpile,' she was sure she heard someone say, and felt breath in her ear.

Freya spun around. There was no one behind her.

'The woodpile,' the voice repeated. As soon as the words were said, a wind whipped past Freya. She stumbled backwards. But all was quiet again. All was still.

'The woodpile!' Freya called out. She tried to run in the direction of the woodland where she had last heard Callum's voice. The snow was so thick she could hardly see. 'Callum!' she called. 'The woodpile. Have you tried the wood pile?'

She stopped and listened. She could have punched the air when she heard the cracking of branches. A figure emerged from the darkness.

'Freya!' Callum called. 'What did you say?'

'The woodpile,' she said. 'Have you tried looking for Jasper at the woodpile?'

Callum looked down at her as though he thought she had gone a little crazy. Even so, he turned and pushed through the snow along the back of the house. Freya followed. At the end of the house, a brick wall ran parallel to the side of the house. Freya could just make out a dark shed-like lean-to construction against the wall, its roof covered in snow.

'Jasper?' Callum called.

A faint whimper came from the direction of the lean-to.

'Jasper?' Callum called again, picking up his pace, Freya still following.

They saw the shape at the same time. A scruffy terrier, sitting in the snow amongst the logs stacked in the lean-to, shaking and whimpering.

'Oh my god,' Callum said, scooping Jasper up in his arms. 'What were you thinking running off like that?' Callum unbuttoned his waistcoat and tucked the shivering dog inside so that Jasper's head was on a level with his own.

'How's he doing?' Freya asked when she took two fresh cups of coffee into the housekeeper's parlour and placed them on the table. Callum was sitting on the floor before the fire, rubbing Jasper's damp fur with a towel.

'He doesn't seem to be any the worse for his adventure,' Callum said. He rubbed the dog's head vigorously. 'I should have fixed that latch myself rather than waiting for the handyman to come back.'

Freya placed one of the cups of coffee on the hearth beside Callum's knee. She took a seat in one of the armchairs. 'Don't be so hard on yourself,' she said. 'It was an accident. You didn't know the wind was going to catch it.'

Callum placed the dog bed before the fireplace. Jasper jumped in and after turning a few circles, curled into a nose-to-tail ball. Callum tucked a clean blanket around the dog. He sat on the rug and collected the coffee. With his elbows resting on his knees, he kept one hand on Jasper and took a sip. 'We have you to thank for finding him. I'd gone in the completely wrong direction. I've never known him go towards the walled garden before. What made you think to look there?'

Freya took a slow sip of her coffee. 'I just thought, you know, sticks and dogs. Logs are just like big sticks really, aren't they? And a house like this always has lots of logs for the fires.' She was hardly convincing herself, but Callum had no reason not to believe her odd and improbable explanation.

'Well, it was inspired.' Callum got to his feet. 'Keep an eye on him for a minute, would you?' He left and Freya watched Jasper's chest rise and fall beneath the blanket. The lie she had just told Callum was definitely a fib she couldn't take back. If she tried to explain she had only known where to find Jasper because she'd heard a disembodied voice, he would think she had gone well and truly round the twist. A coal spat and slipped through the grate. With the glow of the lights on the Christmas tree in the corner and the fire in the hearth, she felt even more festive than she had earlier.

'I thought we could use this,' Callum said. He placed two glasses and a decanter on the table. Pouring a large slug of the amber liquid into each glass, he handed one to Freya. She placed her cup of coffee on the side table.

'It's medicinal,' Callum said, chinking his glass to Freya's before sitting in the armchair opposite her.

He took a drink and Freya copied him. The brandy swirled down her throat, warming her insides as it went.

'My mother swears by a drop of brandy when you've had a shock,' Callum said.

'Are you all right?' Freya asked.

'I am now that he is home safe and sound. Look at him there, fast asleep with no clue to the panic he caused.'

Freya took another sip of the brandy, watching Callum watch Jasper.

'May I ask you a question?' Freya said. 'About the Mandevilles?'

'Of course,' Callum said, relaxing back into his chair.

'It's about the history of the Mandevilles really. I just

wondered whether there was a daughter called Imogen at any point.'

'Imogen...' Callum said, rolling his glass around in his hands. 'Imogen.'

'I think she might have been a twin,' Freya said.

Callum thought for a moment. 'I think there was a set of twins. In the early 1800s. Sisters of the baronet. I'm pretty sure there's a painting of them as children in the library.'

'And do you know what became of her?'

Callum shrugged. 'Afraid not. It's not a name that comes up on the tours the Mandevilles and their volunteers give. There might be some of her history in the books in the library. If I'm honest, we know more about the baronets than their siblings. Especially sisters and female relatives. It was a less enlightened time. Any reason you wanted to know about this Imogen?'

Freya took a sip of her brandy. 'Not really,' she said. 'I think I read about her somewhere, so I was curious.' She could hardly say that she thought she had met her earlier in the day and was certain it was Imogen's voice that had whispered to her outside in the snow so they knew where to find Jasper.

A snore came from the basket before the fire. Freya laughed along with Callum. 'I think that's an alarm of sorts telling us it's time to turn in.' Callum said. 'It's the big day tomorrow. I can show you where your room is. You'd be welcome to come back down and enjoy more brandy. But I have an early start.'

'I'd like to turn in too, if that's okay,' Freya said.

'We won't worry about washing the glasses and coffee things,' Callum said. 'I'll be up early and can do them then.'

'If you're sure,' Freya said.

As soon as Callum got up from his chair, Jasper leapt from his bed as though he hadn't been asleep at all. He stretched while Callum placed a guard before the fire and turned out first the Christmas tree lights and then the lamps. 'Look at him,' Callum said. 'Like butter wouldn't melt.'

Freya followed Callum and Jasper from the parlour. Callum

double checked the back door was secure. He turned the lights off as they went, with Jasper's claws tip-tapping along the flagged floor of the basement corridor. At the top of the stone steps, they turned left in the network of whitewashed staff passageways. Freya followed Callum up a staircase lit by unshaded bulbs.

'It's not quite as grand as the staircase in the hallway,' Callum said over his shoulder. They came to a landing, and he pointed to a door. 'That goes out to the first-floor bedrooms of the family and guests,' he said. They continued up and came to another landing where the stairs finished. They seemed to be in an attic space. The roof was slanted with windows at regular intervals. Opposite the windows doors ran the length of the corridor with its varnished floorboards.

Coming to a stop with Jasper at his heels, Callum said, 'We're up in the cheap seats here.' He laughed and then added, 'Not really. But we are up where the staff have always lived. The Mandevilles have always made it comfortable for the people who work for them. The rooms were all made up the day before yesterday ready for the staff coming back from their holidays.'

'I don't want to take someone's room without asking,' Freya said.

'It's not a problem. We always make up a few spare, especially when there's a big party on. Some of the guests may suddenly decide to stay so they find their way up here for the night if the bedrooms downstairs are all taken.'

He opened the door to the room closest to the stairs. 'This is one of the emergency guest rooms.' He moved aside. Freya stepped into a room with a single bed with a metal bedstead opposite a fire-place, a dark wooden wardrobe and a matching nightstand. A few books and ornaments lined a shelf. The pink floral bedspread matched the curtains and a green rug covered all but the very edges of the varnished floorboards.

'It's beautiful,' Freya said. 'Like something out of an old-fash-ioned children's book.'

'But with the added benefit of central heating,' Callum said, nodding to the radiator. 'I hope you'll be warm enough up here. There are extra blankets and eiderdowns in the cupboards out on the landing if you're cold. The bathroom's the third door down. You'll find new toiletries in the cabinet in there. And clean towels on the rail. It was stocked up in case they're needed for the party.'

'Thank you,' Freya said. 'It's perfect.'

Callum seemed to hesitate for a second or two. 'I hope you don't think this odd, but I came up earlier and put a few bits of clothes in the wardrobe in case you wanted something to sleep in. It's just some joggers and a sweatshirt of mine. They're clean.'

Freya turned to look at him. 'Thank you so much,' she said.

'You're very welcome.' Callum smiled. He held her gaze for a moment. 'Anyway,' he said. 'I should let you get on. Just so you know, there's a door halfway up the corridor. It used to separate the men's and women's bedrooms, with only the housekeeper holding the key. It locks from this side, so feel free to lock it if you want to. The door to this room also locks from the inside. I'm right down at the other end of the house if you need anything.'

Freya was about to thank him again but was stopped by Jasper trotting into the room. He jumped onto the bed, turned around twice, and curled into a ball.

'Come here, boy,' Callum said. 'I'm sure Freya doesn't want you on her bed tonight.'

Jasper didn't move.

'I don't mind,' Freya said. 'If you don't mind your dog sleeping on someone else's bed.'

'Oh,' Callum said. 'Jasper's not my dog. He belongs to the Mandevilles. He's been entrusted to my care while they're visiting their friends. He doesn't like being away from the house so it's easier for them to leave him here. And he's generally good company. If he's not running away or chucking me over for the company of someone else.' He smiled at the dog. 'But he's made his mind up where he wants to sleep tonight. If you're sure you don't mind.'

'I don't mind at all.' Freya looked to the snow still falling outside the window. 'Do you really think it will melt overnight?'

'If it doesn't, we have plenty in the fridge to keep us going. Right,' Callum said, bringing his palms down onto his thighs. 'I should be going. Do you have everything you need?'

Freya nodded.

'If you're up before me, help yourself to anything you fancy for breakfast,' Callum
said.

'Thank you,' Freya said.

'Good night, Freya.'

'Good night, Callum.'

Freya held the handle of the door. She heard footsteps on the floorboards. When she heard a door click, she looked out. The door halfway down the corridor was half glazed. She watched Callum make his way along the corridor beyond the door until the light was turned off and he disappeared.

Stepping back into the room, Freya kept hold of the door handle. So many feelings rushed at her. She felt winded. Just that morning, that man along the corridor had been little more than a handsome stranger. But now? She opened the wardrobe and found two items of clothing on a shelf above the hanging rail. She took them down. A grey sweatshirt and a pair of grey jogging bottoms. Callum's grey sweatshirt. And Callum's grey jogging bottoms. She placed them on the bed and after checking that Jasper was still sleeping, closed the door and went along the corridor to the bathroom.

The cabinet above the sink was stacked with toiletries and she took out a soap, new toothbrush and toothpaste. After cleaning her teeth, she had a wash.

Back in the bedroom, Freya placed her phone on the nightstand. Stripping off, she shook out her t-shirt and trousers. She took hangers from the wardrobe and hung her clothes on a hook behind the door to air. She looked down at Callum's clothes. Carefully unfolding them, she stepped first into the joggers. They were too long, so she turned them up and had to pull the drawstring at the waist tight to stop them falling down. Picking up the sweatshirt, she pulled it over her head, slipped her arms inside the sleeves and let it come to rest on her body. It was soft as though it had been worn hundreds of times. And each of those times, it had been pressed to Callum's body.

Freya closed her eyes. She lifted the collar of the sweatshirt to her nose and breathed in. She hadn't been close enough to Callum to know if he smelled of cologne or aftershave. But holding the collar of his sweatshirt to her nose, it smelled clean and warm. What would he think if he could see her now, smelling his clothes? Would he think her any more round the twist than if she had told him of the voice out in the snow and her vivid dreams in the house? He clearly didn't think of her in the same way that she thought of him. He hadn't asked if she had a partner. He could have joined the dots since she said she was alone at Christmas but if he had been interested, surely he would have asked the question outright to be sure. But then, she hadn't asked if he had a partner. There might be someone up in Scotland for all she knew.

Reaching out her hand, Freya stroked Jasper's head. 'I'm over-thinking again,' she whispered. 'It's what I always do.'

Jasper let out a long sigh.

Freya checked her phone. It was almost ten o'clock. Still quite early but she needed to be up to get on with the cake.

Turning out the light, she slipped beneath the covers. But she didn't turn the key in the lock. She pulled the collar of Callum's sweatshirt up again, so it covered her nose and mouth. She couldn't help herself. And she couldn't help thinking of all the times in the evening and during their tour of the house when Callum had looked at her for a little longer than was necessary. 'Wishful think-ing, Freya, wishful thinking,' she whispered to herself.

With Callum's sweatshirt still pulled over her nose and mouth and the covers up to her chin, Freya looked to the window. She watched the snow falling. Would it be so dreadful if it didn't melt overnight? Would it be so dreadful if it was just her and Callum alone for a little longer? She thought back to how he had constantly referred to them as 'us' and 'we' across the day. What a gentleman he had been, reiterating how she could lock the doors. What would he think if had been able to read her thoughts and heard them say that she would much rather have him to warm her than an extra eiderdown from the cupboard out in the hall?

Freya's eyes began to close. She saw the warm glow of fairy lights on Christmas trees around the house. The paperchains sway. The lametta sparkle. She smelled the cinnamon and nutmeg and marzipan. She saw a smile. Heard a laugh. Saw the chaos of flour and pastry in a kitchen. And she saw the kissing bough above the door in the hallway.

THIRTEEN

Freya woke to the sound of scratching. She tried to see but it was so dark. There were no streetlights outside the window. No glow from the standby light on the television in the corner of her bedroom.

Scratch, scratch

Scratch, scratch

She sat up, trying to make sense of the shapes in the darkness. She fumbled for the lamp on her nightstand. It wasn't there. She patted the nightstand and found her phone, then pressed the button on the side of the screen to bring it to life. She wiped her eyes. She wasn't in her own room. Of course, she wasn't; she was in Hill House. In the charming room in the attic with about the most comfortable bed she had ever slept in. She nudged the end of the bed with her foot. No dog. Turning the screen to light up the door, she saw Jasper sitting there, looking at her. She checked the time on her phone. Two thirty in the morning. Of course it was. 'You don't need a pee, do you?' she said.

Jasper scratched the door again.

'Okay, okay,' she said. Kicking back the covers, she got out of bed and turned on the light. Jasper didn't move. Just stared at the door. With any luck, he just wanted to go down the corridor to

Callum's room. Freya looked down at herself dressed in Callum's clothes and barely held in a smile. Jasper scratched the door again.

'Okay, okay,' Freya said. 'I take the hint.'

She opened the door and Jasper trotted outside. She'd left the light on in her side of the corridor in case she needed to get up to the loo in the night. She squinted at the bright bulb and watched Jasper head for the stairs.

'No,' she whispered. 'You want to go that way. To Callum's room.'

If Jasper heard her, he chose to ignore her. He was already down the first couple of steps before she reluctantly followed him with her arms wrapped around her waist against the cold. She was pretty sure she had seen a lead hanging up beside the back door. There was no way she was going to let him outside to pee unless there was no chance he would run off into the snowy night again. She looked down at her bare feet. Hopefully there was a pair of Wellies too.

She switched on the lights at the top of the staircase and followed Jasper down the first flight. He didn't seem in a particular rush. At a turn in the stairs, she could see the small landing Callum had shown her that led to the family bedrooms. And she saw that Jasper had stopped at the narrow door which led away from the staff stairs and into the family's part of the house. Jasper sat at the door while she walked down the stairs. She was just a few steps from him when he nudged the door with his nose.

'No!' Freya said. 'We're going down to the basement so you can go out.'

She picked up her pace, but it was no good. The door must have been on the latch as it swung open and Jasper trotted through. Freya ran down the last couple of steps. He could go anywhere in the family side of the house once through there and she would have no chance of finding him. She stepped through the door and instantly felt the difference in flooring. Gone were the cold hard stairs and she stood on a rich scarlet carpet. Thankfully a few dim wall lights lit a long corridor with doors leading away. No doubt to many bedrooms. Freya looked down the corridor but there was no sign of Jasper. She looked to her left and realised she was at the head of the grand staircase stretching down into the hallway. The lights on the Christmas tree in the hall beside the fireplace had been left on and she could just make out Jasper sitting on the top stair. He looked at her for all the world like he was waiting for her.

'You wanted to take the scenic route,' Freya whispered. 'Rather than the staff route. You're not daft, are you?'

Jasper turned and began trotting down the stairs. Freya followed him, her feet sinking into the thick scarlet carpet. She let her palm glide along the highly polished handrail of the bannister, feeling like Kate Winslet sweeping down the stairs in Titanic. She smiled at the memories of the many times she had sat with Grandma to watch one of her favourite films. Always with a box of chocolates and a box of tissues. She was just a few steps from the bottom when she saw not Leonardo DiCaprio waiting for her, but Jasper. 'Good boy,' she whispered. 'Maybe we can sneak you a midnight feast of ham from the fridge once you've done your business.'

Freya took the final step, preparing for her bare foot to make contact with the cold tiles. But as her foot pressed to the floor, she was dazzled by light. She closed her eyes. All her other senses came to life. She heard music and voices, so many voices. Smelled open fires, woodsmoke, perfumes and the scent of delicious food. Felt fine fabric against her skin and the press of her foot into a shoe.

Freya opened her eyes. Jasper was gone. The Christmas tree was gone. Thick evergreens decorated the mantelshelf. Flames leapt in the grate around a large log wrapped in hazel twigs. So many people filled the hallway. Women in fine silks and rich fabrics of shades of all colours; pinks, jades, reds and yellows. A couple of women wore turbans, but most wore their hair back from their faces, their ringlets or curls decorated with headdresses or feathers to complement each dress, some half the height again of the woman who wore them. One or two women wore their sleeves long, but most wore dresses with low necklines, and each woman wore white gloves past their elbows and jewels at their necks, strings of pearls, gold and silver chains. Younger women gossiped and laughed behind fans held to their faces. They were dressed in pastels with more modest jewellery of small crosses, and with ribbons in their hair.

Men congregated in groups, laughing and talking loudly. They wore fine jackets of deep blues and greens and blacks, over shirts with high collars, breeches of a pale linen colour and soft dancing shoes. Soldiers of the regiment – the object of scrutiny of many of the younger women – wore rich red jackets adorned with gold braid that appeared to shine in the candlelight. Guests spilled into the dining room where a huge feast was laid out. Roasted meats served by footmen in powdered wigs, fine sweet treats of marzipan and sugared biscuits. Abundant fruits filled bowls and chargers – apples, oranges, grapes, figs and splendid pineapples.

A small queue waited to have their glasses filled from a ladle in a vast bowl of red-coloured punch. The finest silver cutlery and crystal glasses glistened on tables laid with pristine white cloths and silver candelabras to light the magnificent spectacle. Small groups of people sat at tables in the billiard room, playing cards and games. Cheering or groaning at wins and losses. Footmen moved between the guests in every room, replenishing glasses with wine. Maids offered platters of food while avoiding the children running between the older guests in a high-spirited game of chase, dressed as miniature versions of the adults.

Laughter and chatter filled the air, mixing with music from the ballroom. Pianoforte, violin, cello and flute played lively tunes with vigour and enthusiasm matched by the vigour and enthusiasm of the guests who danced beneath the two vast chandeliers, the candles flickering brightly, lighting the crystal drops. Perfumes and colognes thick with rosewater, bergamot and orange filled the air.

Freya stood at the bottom of the stairs, gripping the bannister. Had she slept through a whole day and stepped into the Mandeville's recreation of a Regency Twelfth Night ball?

'There you are, Freya,' a familiar voice called.

A young woman pushed her way through the throng of people, apologising all the way for bumping into them. She stopped at the bottom of the stairs and took hold of Freya's hands.

'I am so happy to see you,' Imogen said, squeezing Freya's hands tightly.

'Oh! And I, you,' Freya said. In the midst of this... whatever this was... it was good to see someone she knew or at least thought she knew. If it was possible, Imogen looked even more beautiful than when they had first met. She wore a dress so yellow that it seemed gold. A thread ran through it that made it shimmer. It was cut and fitted to perfection. Her hair was worn back with curls before both ears. A white braid wrapped around her hair was decorated with small white flowers that perfectly matched her pristine white gloves.

'You look beautiful,' Freya said.

'As do you,' Imogen said.

Freya looked down at herself. She wore a dress of a pale green, cut as Imogen's was, gathered in below the bust. She ran her fingers over the soft fabric. She put her hands to her hair. It was pulled back and she could feel a braid wrapped about the curls.

'Come with me,' Imogen said. 'Before Mother sees us and makes me go elsewhere with her.'

Imogen led Freya further up the hallway and through a door below the staircase, to the left of where Captain Thomas' portrait should have hung. Imogen brought them to a stop in a corridor with a much lower ceiling than the rest of the house. She closed the door behind them so that the sound of the music and voices softened.

'Mother will never come in here,' Imogen said in a whisper. 'I don't believe she has ever been in these rooms. The staff use them for storage and the estate manager's office is at the end. Nobody will find us in there.'

Freya followed Imogen to a small office with a dark wooden desk and two chairs before an unlit fireplace. It was plain compared to the rest of Hill House with boxes and ledgers filling the shelves running the length of two of the walls.

'Shall we sit?' Imogen said. And then immediately said, 'No, I am too excited to sit.'

'What is it?' Freya asked. She stood beside the desk while Imogen paced up and down the small room. 'What has happened?' Freya tried again.

'I have been thinking since we spoke earlier,' Imogen said. 'Oh, Freya.' She stopped and took Freya's hands again. 'You are the first person I have spoken to in the last six months that has made me feel that I can do something with my life. That I don't need to simply go along with the plans that my mother has plotted for me.'

'I'm not sure I said anything of use,' Freya said.

Imogen let Freya's hands slip and began pacing again. 'But you did. You made me think about my grandmother. Talking to you about your own grandmother and knowing that someone else felt the same as me made me truly reflect on the advice my grandmother would have given to me now. I know she is not with me in person. But in spirit she is. Her spirit lives on in me. What are we if not the living embodiment of those who have gone before? I thought about what she would think of how I have been feeling and behaving recently. It is as though I have surrendered. I was on the verge of giving up what is important to me.'

Imogen came to a stop. 'Well, I won't do it. I simply won't. Mother may present me if she wants. I shall receive suitors with good grace and manners. I will not shame my family. But I will not marry a single one of them. There is only one man for me. Arthur Richmond. If I have to wait until I am of age to take him, then so be it. We could go to Scotland to marry now, but I know my grandmother would not want me to tarnish the name of my family. And I would not do that to Rebecca and Tris. And don't you see, I have my inheritance from my grandmother. I have spoken to Arthur at length about how best we can use it when I am married to establish institutions that will really help people. He is in complete agreement with me. And our thoughts are as one.'

'You've clearly given it a great deal of thought,' Freya said. 'But I don't think I can take any credit.'

'But, don't you see? This is all thanks to you. Until we spoke today, I really was thinking that the best thing in the long run would be to do my mother's bidding. Arthur is handsome and good and would have had no trouble in finding another bride. But I had an opportunity to talk to him this afternoon and he is prepared to wait as I am. I explained that I had spoken to someone who had made me believe the life I want to lead is possible.'

'I'm so glad, Imogen,' Freya said. She imagined the young woman who had fallen out of the history of her family so that she had become just the sister of the baronet. Imogen was a woman in her own right. She should be remembered as such. Even if this was an hallucination or a dream, she couldn't just stand by and let Imogen give up without a fight.

'You have to do what you want with your life, Imogen,' Freya said. 'You'll have to be strong for the next few years, but if anyone can do it, I know it's you. You know how best to handle your mother.'

Imogen puffed out her cheeks. 'She won't like it. But I'm sure Rebecca will find a husband when we are presented, which should keep mother occupied for a while. And then there is the prospect of grandchildren. I am sure if I try to cause her no trouble and try not to cost my parents anything, she will have more than enough to direct her thoughts away from me.'

Freya took hold of Imogen's hands. 'You are a strong determined woman. Remember, you have the strength of your grandmother in you. You can do anything you set your mind to. Arthur Richmond is lucky to have you.'

Imogen smiled and gripped Freya's hands. 'What about you, Freya?' she said. 'What about your Callum?'

Freya hadn't been expecting that question. She shook her head. 'He's not *my* Callum.'

'But you would like him to be?' Imogen said.

Freya thought to the man who had spoken to her that evening.

Who had confided in her about being homesick for his family. Who had offered to help her find a new home. Who had made her dinner in a chaos of flour and pastry. 'I would,' she said.

Imogen looked Freya up and down. 'I wish Callum was here to see you this evening. I have never known a more beautiful woman. On the outside, yes, but on the inside too.'

'I'm not sure...' Freya said.

'Well, I am,' Imogen said. 'Callum makes your heart sing. You said so earlier. You must give voice to that song so that he knows how you feel.' Imogen paused and laughed. 'Do you think me very immature for thinking and saying such things?'

'No,' Freya said. 'I think you talk a lot of sense.'

'Good!' Imogen said. 'It's time for both of us to find happiness again. It's what our grandmothers would have wanted.'

'Are you sure you're only seventeen?' Freya said. 'You have more wisdom than women twice your age.'

'I have been counselled by very wise women,' Imogen said. She leant forward and kissed Freya on the cheek. 'And I feel as though I have known you my whole life, rather than just one day. Thank you, Freya. For helping me see what I must do. And you too will be happy. I can see it in your eyes.' She let go of Freya's hands and brushed down her dress. 'Now, I must return to the ball before Mother misses me. I will dance with whoever my mother wants me to, but all the while I will think of Arthur. And when mother is not watching, I will smile at him. And we have already agreed that a smile is as good as a dance. No, it is better.'

Freya followed Imogen from the office and down the corridor. At the door, Imogen stopped. 'I believe that you are leaving in the morning,' she said. 'Father says your brother is sending a carriage for you. But if there is ever anything I can do to help you,' she said. 'Then you must let me know. Send me a letter or visit me if you can. I will always be so grateful to you for helping me remember what my life is for.'

'Thank you,' Freya said. Who knew if she would ever see Imogen again. And if she didn't, she wanted to leave Imogen with no doubt about how she felt about her. 'Earlier you wondered whether we could be friends, even though there is a difference in our ages. Well, I can't think of anyone who I would want as a friend more than you.'

Imogen smiled. 'And I you, Freya. And I shall leave you with this thought. It is Epiphany tomorrow. And my grandmother always said that every 6th January is the chance to start again and do something new. The past cannot be changed but the future is ours to shape. I've had my Epiphany. It's your turn now.'

Imogen opened the door, and they stepped out into the throng of the party.

'You must try the marchpane fruits in the dining room,' Imogen said over the noise. 'They are simply delicious. And they are playing cards in the library if you would like to join a game. The tokens are in the shape of little mother-of-pearl fish, which is apparently all the rage in London this season.'

Freya was about to say goodbye when Imogen took her hand again. She began leading her to the ballroom. 'Oh, no,' Freya said. 'I can't dance.'

'I don't believe that for a single second,' Imogen said. 'And you must dance. It is a party, after all!' Imogen picked up her pace and Freya had no choice but to follow.

They were soon swallowed up by other guests making their way into the ballroom. Candles glittered in the two huge chandeliers. The crystal drops captured the light from every tiny flame and shone it about the room. More candles glowed from gold sconces lining the walls, picking out the details of the gold moulding running around the walls and ceiling. Guests filled every space in their clothes of every colour. Barely an inch of floorboard was visible around the men lined up on one side and the women on the other, preparing to start a dance of which they all knew the steps.

Imogen stopped in the line with Freya beside her. 'I really don't know what to do,' Freya said as the music struck up.

'Just copy me,' Imogen said, shouting to be heard over the pianoforte, cello, violin and flute.

Imogen curtseyed to the man opposite her. Freya copied her friend. Summoning every bit of knowledge she could remember from Grandma's period dramas, and keeping an eye on Imogen, Freya copied the steps. The music was lively, but thankfully the steps weren't so complicated that she couldn't follow. Imogen leant into her. 'You should thank me,' she shouted. 'Your partner is Henry Waterford. Every young woman in the county has her eye on him!'

Freya looked to the chap opposite her. With his long dark jacket, linen-coloured breeches, high necked shirt and dark wavy hair, he certainly had a touch of the Mr Darcy about him. Freya laughed just as it was time to step forward. Henry held out his hand. Freya took it and Henry led her in a dance along the line and then back to their original positions. He didn't seem to mind that she got most of the steps wrong. All around the ballroom, guests watched and clapped, tapping their feet in time to the music, rosy-cheeked women fanning their faces against the warmth of so many people in the room. Freya spotted Imogen's sister further down the line and even further down, she saw Arthur Richmond. He danced with a pretty girl but at every opportunity, he looked towards Imogen with more love in his eyes that Freya had ever seen. Imogen was in the midst of dancing with her partner so didn't see Arthur. Freya smiled. Imogen would be all right, she was sure of it.

At the end of the dance, Freya stepped forward and thanked Henry. He was handsome and gracious when he bowed and thanked her. She turned to speak to Imogen but felt something touch her leg. She looked down. Jasper was nudging her ankle with his nose. He sat down, and behind him Freya suddenly saw that the guests had disappeared. The music had stopped. Looking up, she saw the Christmas tree outside in the hallway. The ballroom was in darkness and empty except for her and Jasper. The silence felt louder than the party.

Jasper walked past Freya, trotting out into the hallway. She followed him. Up the grand staircase, through the door on the landing, up the staff stairs to the attic and into the small bedroom.

Jasper jumped on the bed and curled into a ball. Freya closed the door. 'What's happening here?' she said to Jasper, stroking his ears. 'Because that wasn't a dream.'

She looked down at herself. One minute she had been wearing a Regency gown and the next she was in Callum's joggers. Callum. Callum who made her heart sing. Switching out the light, Freya crawled into bed. She watched the snow silently fall outside the window for a few moments before pulling the covers over her head.

FOURTEEN

THE DAY OF THE PARTY

When Freya's alarm went off, she was already awake. The second half of her night's sleep had been disturbed by strange dreams that she forgot as soon as she woke up.

Pushing back the covers, she got up to turn on the light before sitting back on the bed. She stroked Jasper's ears. 'Good morning, boy,' she said. He lifted his head briefly. Freya began replaying the scenes from the ball and stopped. She had to work. And she needed a clear head for the day. Standing up, she looked down at herself. At Callum's sweatshirt and joggers. The thrill at putting them on seemed like such a long time ago, so much had happened between then and now. Freya hit herself on the forehead with the heel of her hand. Really? Had she really been to a Regency ball? Or had it been an elaborate hallucination. Or a dream. Or was that a convenient explanation?

After going to the bathroom for a wash and to brush her teeth, Freya returned to the small room and made the bed. She removed the sweatshirt and joggers. Folding them carefully, she placed them on the pillow and dressed in her work clothes.

'Are you coming?' she said to Jasper. He showed no sign of moving, so she left the room after turning out the light.

She navigated the staff stairs down alone but stopped at the sound of voices coming from the basement kitchens. She looked down at herself. She was still dressed in her t-shirt, work trousers and trainers. Taking a few tentative steps, she reached the head of the stone steps and took the first few down. The door at the end was open and she breathed a sigh of relief when she saw a small army of caterers bringing boxes down. She even recognised a few from the day before yesterday.

'Hello there,' Liz called. 'How's the baking going?'

'Good, thanks,' Freya said.

'We've lots of time to make up what with yesterday,' Liz said. 'Mind. It was nice to have a day off, but good job that snow's melted now. And we're paying for that day off! We're up against it to get everything ready for this evening.'

Freya smiled. 'Same here.'

'The kettle's on already,' Liz said. 'Shall I bring a brew through for you? And a couple of breakfast treats. We always bring plenty when we have an early start.'

'Thanks,' Freya said. 'That's really kind.'

She collected her file from the housekeeper's parlour. Retreating to the pastry room she pulled her apron over her head and tied it at the waist. Callum must have been down early to unlock the back door. She looked at her watch. It wasn't even six o'clock. If the Regency ball felt like a dream, so did yesterday evening with Callum. The snow had melted. Life had returned to normal.

After a few minutes, a cup of tea and a plate of treats was delivered to Freya. She left the door ajar and sat at the table checking her notes, eating her sausage roll and drinking her tea. There was something reassuring in listening to the voices and activity in the kitchen. She didn't want to be alone.

Taking down the Twelfth Night cake, Freya placed it on the table. Carefully, very carefully, she took down the decorations and laid them out on the table. With even more care she transferred the cake onto the silver stand on which it would be presented at the party. She turned to the page in her file with the design for the cake and mixed up a bowl of royal icing by hand to use as a glue. Reluctantly, she closed the door so that she could focus on the process of decorating the cake.

As the sun began to show through the window high in the wall, there was a knock at the door. Freya tried not to show her disappointment that it was Liz. She accepted the offer of another cup of tea and Liz made many appreciative noises at Freya's work on the cake. When she returned with the tea, a couple of her colleagues accompanied her. They wanted to see the cake and stood in the doorway making similar noises of approval.

'We know where to go if we ever want a special cake for a party or a wedding.' Freya heard one of them say as they closed the door and went back to the kitchen.

The smells floating along the corridor all morning made Freya's mouth water as she focused on applying particularly intricate decorations. The concentration meant she wasn't looking to the door every other minute, hoping for a certain person to knock and come in. The seconds turned to minutes and the minutes to hours. And still, he didn't knock.

At midday, Liz invited Freya to join the catering team for lunch. In the kitchen, she sat at the table with a bowl of soup and a sandwich. The conversation flowed. All around dishes were covered with food that was ready for the party and food in the process of preparation.

Noelle the event planner appeared with a clipboard and began giving directions to her staff. 'The dressings for the ballroom are being taken in through the front door to save time,' she said. 'The upstairs team will be able to get in at about two to set the tables. The family is expected mid-afternoon, and the guests will start arriving late afternoon. We'll have to use the backstairs to the ballroom once the guests are here. Oh, and Past Time Bakes, there'll be a table up there for you to display your... well, whatever it is you display. You need to have it all up and ready by six. A couple of the upstairs staff will come down to take the main cake to the ballroom at four.'

Noelle's tone was predictably dismissive, but Freya had too much to do to be bothered by her haughtiness.

Returning to the pastry room, Freya jotted some notes about timings in her file. She stood back and looked at the Twelfth Night cake. It was coming along as planned. There were a few more decorations she could add, but the finishing touches would need to be done when it was in place in the ballroom. Some of the icing sculptures were far too delicate to risk being carried through the house. Freya assembled a box she had brought specially to protect the cake and placed it over the top. It left her enough space on the table for her final bake.

After wiping down the table, Freya weighed out ground almonds and icing sugar and mixed them together in a bowl. She added a spoon of rosewater and some ice-cold tap water and mixed the ingredients together to form a perfumed dough. She scattered a handful of icing sugar onto the marble tabletop, tipped out the marzipan and gave it a light knead, working it with the heel of her right hand. The delicious scents of almond and rose were released with each knead. When she was happy with the texture, she lined a round cake tin with rice paper and pressed in half the marzipan.

Scattering another handful of icing sugar onto the table, she rolled out half the remaining marzipan. She took the box of cutters down from the shelf and selected the heart and star shapes she had used for the gingerbread and Shrewsbury cakes. She pressed them into the flattened marzipan until she had eight of each. She could hear Grandma's voice as she worked. *Try not to waste any of the mixture, Freya. Get that cutter right up to the last one you cut. That's it. You're doing a fantastic job.'*

Freya smiled as she added the leftover scraps of marzipan to the remaining larger lump and gave it all another quick knead. She pinched a small portion of the marzipan and began rolling it between her palm and the tabletop to form a ball. She had just made her twelfth ball when a gentle knock sounded at the door.

'Come in,' she said.

The door opened and two friendly faces looked at her.

'Hello,' Lenny said, her hand still on the doorhandle. 'Stan wanted to come and see how you're getting on.'

Freya wiped her hands on her apron. 'Well, you had both better come in then and I'll show you.'

Stan was first in. He made directly for the table and looked at what Freya was working on. 'Marchpane!' he said. 'Look, Lenny, Miss Harris is making marchpane.'

Lenny joined her friend at the table and looked over the stars and hearts and balls. 'Looks more like marzipan to me,' she said. 'And it smells like it. I helped my mum and nan make it for our Christmas cake.'

'You're both right,' Freya smiled. 'Marchpane is the old name for marzipan.' It was hardly a surprise that Stan knew the historically accurate word for marzipan. Once again, he was dressed in his costume which looked straight out of Regency times. Lenny wore a multicoloured stripey sweater over some bright red cords. 'Are your parents working again today?' Freya asked.

'My nan is,' Lenny said. 'She's a volunteer here. She's helping decorate the ballroom. My mum and dad are going to the party tonight. So they're at home getting ready.'

'How lovely,' Freya said. 'They must be very good friends of the Mandeville's to get such a special invitation.'

'They are,' Lenny said. 'My mum's a trustee or something like that. We're always here.'

'And you, Stan?' Freya said. 'Will your parents be at the party?'

'Oh yes,' he said. 'They will be at the Twelfth Night ball. And my sisters will be there too. I really do believe it is the best night of the year. With all the dancing and food and games. I particularly like the food.'

Stan didn't appear to have much of a poker face as he licked his lips when he looked at the marzipan hearts and stars and balls.

'Would you like one?' Freya asked.

Stan looked to Lenny as though unsure of how to answer.

'I always make extra,' Freya said. 'So it's no trouble. Would you like to choose one each?'

'That's very kind,' Stan said. 'I will let Lenny choose for me.'

The children looked at each other and Stan nodded.

Lenny looked at the marzipan shapes. She chose a heart and held it gently in one hand with her other hand pressed to it. She closed her eyes and smiled. 'These were made with love,' she said, her voice soft and low. 'So much love.'

As she spoke, Stan stared at her face. His gaze never once left her.

Eyes still closed, Lenny nodded. 'You are the one,' she said. 'Oh, and such sadness. Such sadness. But in that sadness, you have done a great kindness. A great service to this family. One good turn,' she nodded. 'One good turn...' she repeated.

'Deserves another,' Stan said, completing his friend's sentence.

At the sound of his voice, Lenny opened her eyes. She blinked and turned to him. In her normal voice, she said. 'Would you like a star, Stan?'

'Yes please,' he nodded enthusiastically.

Collecting a star, Lenny held a treat in each hand. 'Thank you so much, Freya,' she said. 'I love marzipan.'

'Marchpane,' Stan corrected.

'It can be either,' Freya said.

'We'll go now so you can get on,' Lenny said. 'My nan said I shouldn't come down here and disturb people for too long. Otherwise I'll get a reputation for being a nuisance. Thank you again, Freya.' Lenny was halfway to the door when she said Freya's name and was out in the hallway when she shouted, 'It's marzipan!'

Stan charged after her. 'Thank you, Miss Harris,' he called before shouting, 'Marchpane!'

For a few moments more, all Freya could hear were the words

marzipan and marchpane shouted in what seemed to be a contest to see who was louder. She laughed, closed the door and washed her hands. What a strange pair they made. Lenny and Stan. One dressed in the most modern and brightest of colours and the other as though he had just stepped from a costume hire shop. Freya dried her hands. Why Stan asked Lenny to choose everything for him, she didn't know. And they spoke so strangely. Whatever Lenny had been talking about, she had no clue. The children seemed to have a private way of speaking that each of them understood. She was doing the family a service by baking, that was true. And it was sweet of Lenny to say that the marzipan had been made with love. It was probably because she had chosen a heart.

Returning to her bake, Freya made a thin icing paste to stick the decorations to the body of the marzipan cake. The balls decorated the outer edge, and she placed the stars and hearts in the middle. She added some rosewater to the paste and used it as a glaze to brush over the entire cake before putting it in a low oven.

She glanced at her watch. It was almost two o'clock. The cake would need to be in the oven for half an hour. She decided to use the time productively and washed the silver platters she had brought to display all the bakes. After drying them, she carried them out into the corridor, up the stone steps, along the staff passageway and through the door beside the long-case clock.

Voices came from the ballroom and when she entered, Freya found at least a dozen staff laying tables spread out in one half of the ballroom. She looked around, sure her mouth was open. The ballroom had looked beautiful when she had seen it empty but seeing it set for a party was splendid. Staff were busy laying place settings with white china and silver cutlery from wooden canteens. Others were polishing crystal glasses for white wine, red wine and water. At a separate table staff worked on floral centrepieces for each table and to decorate the room with holly, ivy, fronds of fern, pinecones, blue candles and silver ribbons. Throughout the rest of the house, the colour theme for Christmas was gold, red and green, but in here, it was silver and blue. It felt like a magical icy wonderland.

'Are you the cake lady?' one of the members of staff asked.

Freya nodded.

'That's your table over there. Is it all right?'

'Thanks, yes,' Freya said. She placed her platters on the table covered in a pure white tablecloth, positioned just to the side of the dining tables. It was the perfect backdrop for her theme. She looked around and imagined the room she had seen in the wee small hours of the morning. The dancers and the candles. Imogen and Arthur. The music and the food and the games. She pushed the thoughts down. There was nothing else she could do.

Returning to the kitchen, Freya collected the tins of bakes, which she took up to the ballroom and placed on the table. With great care, she carried up the tins containing the final items of decoration for the Twelfth Night cake. She would begin her set up just after four o'clock when the main cake was brought up. If she had to be clear by six, then she would much rather be early than late.

After another three trips, all the tins containing the bakes were on the table in the ballroom. Back in the pastry room, she took the marzipan cake from the oven, slipped it from the tin, and placed it on a rack to cool.

It was almost three o'clock when Freya joined the caterers in the main kitchen for another cup of tea. She was ahead of schedule, so could spare the time. She chatted to the other staff, admiring the aromas of the food they were preparing. There was roast beef and capons. Game pie, buttered vegetables and brown soup. They would be followed by a range of jellies, custards and ice creams with sugared fruits, nuts and cheese and pickled vegetables. It wasn't as vast or elaborate as a Regency banquet, but everything was as authentic as they could make it.

Freya accepted the offer of sampling a couple of the canapés –

smoked salmon served alongside shots of white soup served warm. She enjoyed the company and the food. But in all the time she had spent going up and down to the ballroom and sitting in the main kitchen, she had not seen the person she hoped to see. It was a real possibility that she would not see him again before she left. She would submit her invoice to him by email, and it would be paid without the need for further contact. Freya's heart sank at the thought. She couldn't allow herself to believe it. She needed to be filled with hope so that hopefulness came through in the main cake that she still had to complete. Once or twice, she thought about going back to the pastry room. But there was nothing else to do. She would rattle around in there alone. It would be much better to stay in company and keep her spirits up. And the hope of a chance sighting.

Just before four o'clock, Freya thanked everyone for the tea and hospitality and delicious samples of the banquet and returned to the pastry room. Within minutes, two men from Noelle's team appeared to take the cake up. Freya showed them how to hold it safely. It was something she'd had to do many times, but she couldn't remember a cake ever being so fragile.

To their credit, the two chaps took their time. Under Freya's instruction, they were able to keep the cake level in its box as they carried it up the stairs. There were no guests in the hallway, so they were able to take it through the into the ballroom, saving the need for navigating the precarious staff passages that ran behind the ballroom.

With the cake positioned in the centre of the tablecloth, Freya carefully removed the cardboard frame and box she had constructed to keep it safe. She smiled as she took the last of the cardboard away. The cake had made the journey unscathed. With her file open to the page of her design and the tins of decorations open and ready, Freya put on a pair of catering gloves and began the delicate process of constructing the decoration on the top of the cake. Gently, very gently, she eased the fragile pieces into place. She was pretty sure she held her breath each time she lowered one onto the cake. After placing the final piece on top, she stepped back and looked. It was better than she could have hoped for.

'Looking good!' one of the chaps laying the tables called.

It was a joy and a breeze to set the rest of the table. Putting out the platters, Freya laid out the gingerbread, Shrewsbury cakes and Rout cakes. She carefully constructed a pyramid of mince pies. There was just the marzipan cake to bring up and put on the empty platter.

'Just over there,' she heard someone say. She looked up to see a woman directing musicians to the space at the very end of the room. She wore a sweater and jeans and comfortable looking trainers. 'After you've set up, just give me a shout and I'll take you down to the kitchen for a good feed before you start.' The woman turned to Freya. 'Blimey!' she said. 'Look at all that!'

She joined Freya at the bake table.

'Would you believe it!' the woman said. 'And you've done all that yourself?'

Freya nodded.

'Maureen,' the woman said. 'Maureen Arnold. I'm a volunteer here. I'm doing a bit of herding of people around for the party tonight.'

'Freya,' Freya said. 'Freya Harris.'

'Ah,' Maureen said. 'So you're the lovely lady from the pastry room my granddaughter has been telling me all about. She couldn't say enough good things about the icing and marzipan you gave to her. Thank you for being so kind. I'm sure she must get a bit bored rattling about here in her Christmas holidays with me when her mum and dad are working. But she's just that bit too young to go to her friend's house like her sister. I hope she didn't make a nuisance of herself.'

'Not at all,' Freya said. 'Lenny and Stan were perfectly well behaved.'

'Stan?' Maureen said.

'Her little friend,' Freya said.

'You've got me there,' Maureen said. 'I've never heard of a Stan.'

'Oh,' Freya said. 'He could be the son of one of the caterers.'

'You're probably right,' Maureen said. 'My little Leonora is a friendly soul. She's always making little chums.'

'Leonora?'

'Sorry, Lenny. She's taken to shortening it, but I'm so used to using her full name. Anyway, I should let you get on. But I can tell you one thing, Lady Mandeville is going to be thrilled with what you've done there. I don't think they were expecting anything like it.'

A phone rang and Maureen took it from the bag she held over her shoulder. She looked at the screen. 'It's my daughter. I should take it. She's a bit flustered about her dress for this evening! It was lovely meeting you, Freya.'

'And you, Maureen,' Freya said.

As Maureen walked away, Freya heard her say. 'Lou? What's that? I can hardly hear you. You know the signal here is terrible. I'm sure you look beautiful. You always look beautiful.'

FIFTEEN

With the setup finished in the ballroom and the marzipan cake in its place on the table, Freya tidied the pastry room. She washed down surfaces, mopped the floor and cleaned the sink. Grandma had always said they should leave a workplace in as good – if not better – order than when they started. She mopped in the corners and thought about Maureen talking to her daughter. It's how Grandma would have spoken to her. And the thought of it made her smile. The thought of Lenny and Stan made her smile too. Freya paused and leant on the mop. They had behaved like best friends who had known each other forever when it would seem they had only just met. So, it was possible to form an attachment and closeness to someone you had known for only a matter of days.

Freya started mopping again. There had still been no sign of him. She took her phone from her pocket. No messages. As she scrubbed the marble table, she watched caterers carry trays of canapés towards the stone steps. They had changed into smart black trousers with white shirts and black waistcoats. Freya pictured a dog tucked inside a waistcoat against the cold. A tweed waistcoat.

With the cleaning finished, Freya accepted an invitation to join some of the caterers in the housekeeper's parlour. They were taking a break and having a bite to eat. She had packed up her equipment and could be loading it into the car right now. Her services were no longer needed, and she could collect her platters and cake stand in the morning. That's how it usually worked. She had no reason to stay. But she told herself that something might happen to the Twelfth Night cake and she might be needed to see to it.

Through the open door, she watched course after course carried from the main kitchen and along the corridor. She sat through changes in the catering shifts and different people coming into and leaving the parlour as their breaks began and ended. Those that had been upstairs overflowed with details of the party. The food, the decorations, the fabulous music. And the outfits. Oh, the outfits! Everyone had made a huge effort to dress in the style of the Regency era.

At around nine o'clock the chap acting as maître d' appeared in the parlour.

'Miss Harris,' he said to Freya. 'You are Miss Harris, aren't you?'

'Yes,' Freya said.

'Excellent,' the man said. 'Lady Mandeville would like to see you in the ballroom.'

'I beg your pardon?' Freya said.

The man smiled. 'It's nothing bad. Come on, Lady Mandeville says she can't allow the dancing to start until she has spoken to you.'

Freya stood up. She turned to Liz. 'How do I look?' she asked. 'Should I take my apron off.'

'I wouldn't,' Liz said. 'It's your uniform. You wear it with pride. You might want to smooth your hair down a bit at the back. That's it. You look great.'

Freya followed the maître d' along the basement corridor, up the stone steps, along the staff passageway. Even before they stepped into the hallway, Freya heard voices raised in enjoyment. She smelled perfumes and colognes. Heard the chink of decanter against glass. There was even the faint smell of cigars and cigarettes coming from the billiard room. She looked up into the kind eyes of Captain Thomas Mandeville. Whoever Lady Mandeville was, she was related to him in some way and Freya hoped that she would be just as kind as Captain Thomas seemed to be.

Freya stepped into the ballroom behind the maître d', but he instantly stepped aside. 'Lady Mandeville,' he said. 'I would like to introduce Miss Freya Harris.'

Freya felt the eyes of everyone at every table turn to look at her. By her reckoning, that was at least forty people, not counting the waiting staff and the band.

'Miss Harris!' A woman said, getting up from a table. Freya was struck momentarily dumb. The woman wore a Regency style dress, nipped in below the bust with the swell of her cleavage above a square neckline. The dress was so yellow that it was almost gold, and her hair was pulled back with just two ringlets before her ears. All around men were dressed in long tailcoats with high necked shirts and women in silks, some with feathers in their hair. It wasn't until she saw the woman's face that Freya believed she wasn't Imogen. She was as beautiful, but at least a decade older.

'Please don't be embarrassed,' Lady Mandeville said, standing before Freya. 'But we just had to ask you to come up. Your creations have been the talk of the evening, and I couldn't let it pass without thanking you.'

Freya looked towards the table. What she had created was a cake decorated to celebrate the Mandevilles. The base of the cake was decorated with replicas of the gates of Hill House in filigree icing. On the top, she had fashioned two lions holding aloft a globe. They stood upright, supported from behind. The inspiration had come from the research she had been able to undertake quickly after receiving the commission. The filigree hearts and stars around the lions symbolised the love and hope there should always be in a home. And the theme of stars and hearts was replicated in the cakes and biscuits she had baked.

'As I understand it, a Twelfth Night cake should be a showstopper,' Lady Mandeville said. 'I can honestly say, you have delivered that and so much more. Thank you for making the centrepiece of our party so wonderful.'

'It was my pleasure,' Freya said.

'Please everyone, let's give Miss Harris a round of applause.'

Freya looked around as everyone applauded. She had to hold back tears. It had been a long day, a long couple of days. And to be showered with praise for her first solo project was almost too much to bear. She nodded her head by way of thanks but couldn't speak.

'It seems a shame to cut into, but cut it we must,' Lady Mandeville said. 'How else will we find who has the bean and pea and who will be king and queen for the rest of the evening?'

The maître d' handed Lady Mandeville a knife and she made the first cut. A member of staff stepped forward to cut the cake into pieces.

The conversations started again. The band struck up Regency music played on piano, violin, cello and flute.

'Would you like me to walk you out?' the maître d' asked Freya.

'No, thank you,' she said. 'I can make my own way down.'

SIXTEEN

Out in the hallway, Freya had to pause below the staircase. She wiped her eyes on the back of her hand. They were tears, but they were happy tears. She hadn't expected that reaction. There had been lots of thank-yous over the years for cakes, but never one in a ballroom with everyone dressed as though they had stepped from the pages of a Jane Austen novel. Music floated into the hallway along with the sound of people talking in raised voices and laughing.

'Hello,' a voice said.

Freya turned to find one of the guests standing behind her. The woman wore a Regency style dress in a beautiful midnight blue. Her hair was simply pulled back with no feather or adornments. She looked strangely familiar, as though they had met somewhere, although Freya couldn't place her.

'You're Freya, aren't you?' the woman said.

'That's right,' Freya said.

'Your cake is a triumph,' the woman said. 'Lady Mandeville is thrilled.'

'Thank you,' Freya said.

'Sorry,' the woman said with a little laugh. 'I should have introduced myself. I'm Louisa. Lou.'

The penny dropped. 'Oh,' Freya said. 'I thought there was something about you that looked familiar. I met your mum earlier.'

Louisa smiled. 'She said. And I think my daughter has been pestering you for treats while you've been here.'

Freya laughed. 'I don't mind. It was nice to have visitors down in the pastry room.'

'Visitors?' Louisa said, emphasising the 's' at the end of the word.

'Lenny and Stan.'

'Leonora was with someone?'

'I think he must be the son of one of the caterers,' Freya said. 'They got along very well. He had an interesting dress sense though. He wore an outfit that wouldn't have looked out of place in the ballroom at the party.'

Louisa seemed to think for a moment. 'Ah,' she said with a smile. 'I think I know who you mean. Little boy. Blond hair. Scarlet tailcoat.'

'That's the one,' Freya said. 'He was a sweet little chap. But he spoke like he had just walked out of Regency times.'

'He would,' Louisa said.

'Pardon?'

'I just mean that's how he talks.' Louisa paused, as though thinking of how to phrase something. 'Hill House is a very special place,' she said. 'Lots of visitors find what they need here. If they are open to it.'

'I've enjoyed working here for the last few days,' Freya said.

'And has Callum treated you well?'

It was the first time she had heard his name all day and Freya felt her cheeks flush. 'He has,' she said.

Louisa smiled. It was a smile that seemed to say more than the smile itself. 'That's good,' Louisa said. 'Very good. Anyway, I should probably let you get on. I need to get back to the party before I'm missed. I just wanted to say thank you for being kind to Lenny. She was very taken with you. And she is a very good judge of character.'

Freya tried to hide her smile. 'Thank you. Louisa,' she said.

'Lou,' Louisa said, 'my friends call me, Lou.'

Freya watched Louisa turn towards the ballroom. She paused for a couple of seconds before the painting of Captain Thomas Mandeville. She seemed to take a deep breath before carrying on and disappearing around the corner of the staircase.

Freya continued to look in the direction of the ballroom. The apple hadn't fallen far from the tree with Lou. She spoke in the same kind of riddles as her daughter. And they shared a wonderful warm energy.

With the party in the ballroom in full swing, Freya headed for the door at the back of the hall. She was about to step through when half a dozen of the waiting staff appeared, carrying some indistinguishable steaming drinks in little glasses. Freya stepped aside to let them pass and felt someone tap her on her shoulder.

'Hello, stranger.'

Freya closed her eyes and took a deep breath. She turned around slowly.

Callum was standing in the doorway to the library. He leant against the doorframe, his arms folded over his chest. He smiled. 'Where have you been all day?' he asked.

'I've been where I should have been all day,' Freya said, trying not to smile. 'I don't know where you've been.'

Instead of answering, Callum beckoned for her to join him in the library.

They stood just inside the room lined with shelves of books. A dark wooden desk stood in the window with a globe beside it and two comfortable looking armchairs before the fireplace. As with the hallway, many paintings hung on the walls and framed family photographs stood on the shelves in front of books.

'I am in the presence of greatness,' Callum said. 'As I live and breathe, the toast of Hill House is standing before me.'

'What are you talking about?' Freya asked.

'Your cake,' Callum said. 'I know Lady Mandeville called you in to say thank you in front of everyone, but she also asked me to have a quiet word with you.'

'Did I do something wrong?' Freya said.

'On the contrary.' Callum laughed. 'Lady Mandeville has a list of upcoming events and has asked me to see if you would like to come and chat to her next week about producing cakes and treats for them.'

'Are you joking?' Freya said.

'Not at all,' Callum said. 'You make historical themed bakes, and Hill House has historical themed events throughout the year. It's a marriage made in heaven.'

Freya felt her cheeks flush again. 'That... that's great,' she said.

'If you check your calendar for when you're free, I can let Lady Mandeville know.'

'There's nothing in my calendar,' Freya said.

Callum nodded. 'I'll see what works for Lady Mandeville then,' he said. 'And I'm sorry that I wasn't around today. I got involved with salting the approach lane and then sorting the parking for tonight. The snow may have melted but there was still so much to be done.'

'You don't have to explain yourself to me,' Freya said.

'Maybe not,' Callum said. 'But I did want to come and see you. To see how you slept. To see how you were getting on. I thought we might have time to share a coffee before you left. I was looking forward to it.'

A log slipped down the grate in the fireplace, sending a shower of sparks up the chimney. 'I need to chuck another log on,' Callum said. 'Sir Charles has opened a bottle of his best malt for anyone who cares to share a nightcap with him in here after the party. It's a bit of a tradition.'

Freya followed Callum to the hearth. He removed a fireguard and took a log from a wicker basket. He adjusted the fire with a poker and Freya looked around the items on a low table beside the hearth – a framed black and white photograph of a family on a beach, an old-fashioned heavy ashtray, a small dish containing a single item.

'What's that?' she asked Callum.

Getting to his feet, Callum replaced the fireguard and rubbed his hands together, brushing away the dust from the log. He peered at the little item in the dish. 'I can't say I've ever seen it before,' he said. 'It looks like a fish.'

'It is a fish,' Freya said. 'It was a token they used in card games in the Regency era. It's made of mother-of-pearl.'

'I'm impressed at your knowledge,' Callum said.

'Someone told me about them recently,' Freya said. 'That's the only reason I know. But you haven't seen it here before?'

'Can't say I have. Perhaps one of the guests brought it along as part of their costume.'

'Perhaps...' Freya said. She looked down at the fish and scratched the scab on her wrist.

'You've burned yourself,' Callum said.

'What? Oh, it's nothing.'

'We should probably write it up in the accident book.'

'If you say so.'

Freya could feel Callum watching her. 'Are you okay?' he asked.

'Fine. Yes, I'm fine,' she said. She didn't want to look like she was behaving oddly. She looked around so she could make a more normal comment on a mundane object. She raised her eyes to the paintings around the hearth. And stopped. Suspended from a ribbon beside the fireplace were three oval frames containing the portraits of a child and two young women. One of the young women wore a beautiful lilac dress. The young child wore a scarlet jacket. He was painted with a scruffy white and tan terrier sitting at his side. And the second young woman wore a yellow dress that was almost gold. Her hair was pulled back with just a curl in front of each ear.

'You've spotted the famous Mandeville twins,' Callum said. 'And their little brother.'

Staring at the portraits, Freya said, 'What are their names?'

Callum pointed to the pictures in turn. 'That's Rebecca. That's Tristan. And that's Imogen.'

'But... I thought you said you didn't know a Mandeville called Imogen,' Freya said.

'What?' Callum laughed. 'Everyone knows Imogen Mandeville. Or Imogen Richmond as she became when she married. She set up a school for the local children, she established alms houses in the village. Not to mention all the charitable work she did in London with her husband and her sister. I must have thought you were talking about someone else. Lady Mandeville is wearing a recreation of Imogen's dress this evening in honour of her husband's benevolent ancestor.'

Freya still looked at the faces in the portraits. Something had changed. In the space of a day, Imogen's history had altered. And that boy in the painting was Tristan. It made sense now. His sisters called him Tris and Lenny called him Stan. Freya shook her head. What was she trying to tell herself? That she had spent two days down in the pastry room with a little ghost paying her visits?

'Freya?' Callum said.

A knock came at the door. She heard Callum walk to the door and open it. She heard voices. The door closed. Softer footsteps approached her. Something touched her on the shoulder.

'Freya,' a voice said.

Freya spun around.

Lou stood before her. 'I asked Callum to leave us alone for a few minutes,' she said.

Freya searched Lou's face. How could she possibly say that she had seen her daughter with a ghost?

'It takes just one person to make a difference.' Lou said. 'It takes one act to change someone's future.'

Freya still stared at her.

'I don't know what has happened, but I can tell that something has,' Lou said. 'You should know that special things happen in this house.' She took Freya's hands in hers. 'Don't be frightened. It's all good. I promise.'

'Lenny,' Freya said. She glanced over her shoulder at the portraits. 'And Tristan.'

Lou smiled. 'My Lenny has a bit of a gift. But I can see you know that.' She squeezed Freya's hands. 'Sometimes when we need it most, we get the help we need. And sometimes we give others the help they need.'

'One good turn...' Freya said, remembering the words Lenny and Stan had said.

Lou smiled. 'I can see in your eyes that you have a lot of questions. Let everything sink in. But when you need me, I'll be here. There are a few of us who understand.'

'Understand?' Freya said. 'How does anyone understand this?'

'You're very special to this family now. And to this house,' Lou said. 'You'll come to understand it in time. Just as I have.'

Freya stared at Lou again.

'When you're ready, give me a call,' Lou said. 'I don't have all the answers, but I'll answer any question you have as best as I can.' She squeezed Freya's hands again. 'I really should be getting back to the party before I'm missed. Remember contact me any time. Callum has my number.'

Freya felt her hands slip from Lou's. She watched her leave the library, leaving the door ajar.

Freya looked at the painting again of the young woman in the gold dress. It was such a good likeness of the wonderful woman she had met. Because she *had* met her. In the morning room with the windows looking out over the snowy drive. They had spoken in the little office at the end of the corridor under the stairs. She had danced beside her at her family's Twelfth Night ball, and she had seen the young man she loved smile at her. Arthur Richmond. Imogen had married Arthur Richmond.

Freya heard the door creak. She turned to see Jasper standing in the doorway. 'Hello, trouble,' she said. He trotted across the library to her. She bent to stroke his ears. 'At least I know you're real,' she said. She glanced at the dog in the painting with Tristan. With her attention briefly diverted, Jasper sniffed around the low table. Before Freya realised what was happening, he had grabbed the fish token. Once it was in his mouth he made a break for the door.

'Hey!' Freya called. 'You can't take that, Jasper. Jasper!'

When she reached the door, Freya found that Jasper had paused halfway up the hall. 'Jasper,' she whispered. She couldn't go around shouting when there was a fancy party taking place just across the hall in the ballroom. 'Jasper,' she said again. At the sound of his name, he was off again. Freya walked quickly up the hall, not wanting to run in case she was seen. She followed Jasper through the doorway beside the long-case clock and immediately crashed into someone.

'I'm sorry,' she said, without realising who it was.

'Do you know why Jasper had this in his mouth?' Callum said. He held the fish token in his open palm.

'He took it,' Freya said. 'From the bowl in the library.'

'He just trotted through here and dropped it at my feet,' Callum said.

'I'm sorry,' Freya said. 'I shouldn't have let him take it.'

'It's not your fault,' Callum said. 'I have no idea why he would do that.'

They had taken a step away from each other but were still very close in the narrow staff passageway. Freya didn't want to step away any further. And Callum made no sign that he would. He pushed the token into the pocket of his waistcoat. 'I'll put it back later,' he said.

Music floated from the ballroom with the voices and laughter of the guests.

'Sounds like the dancing has started,' Callum said.

Freya nodded, staring at the front of Callum's waistcoat.

'Are you all packed up?' Callum asked.

'Yes. I just need to load my car.'

'The guest room in the attic is still free,' Callum said. 'You'd be more than welcome to stay and drive home tomorrow.'

'I should go...' Freya said.

'I see.' Callum nodded. He brushed his hair away from his face.

'Do you?' Freya said.

Callum looked down at her, a little line between his eyebrows.

'Would you give me a minute?' Freya said. 'I just need to do something.'

'Of course,' Callum said. 'I'll be down in the kitchen if you want to say goodbye before you go.'

Freya nodded. She left the passageway and returned to the library. She closed the door and walked to the fireplace and back again. So many thoughts careered around inside her head. In just two days she had gone from a life without joy, without hope for the future. And now she was wanted. Lady Mandeville wanted to commission her. Freya stopped and shook her head. It was more than that. This house seemed to want her. The people in this house seemed to want her. She paced again, trying to unpick the events. But her thoughts kept taking her back to just one. Stopping at the fireplace, she looked up into the eyes of the young woman in the gold dress. She heard again what Imogen had asked her. *Does he make your heart sing?*

Freya nodded. 'He does, Imogen. He does.'

A draught whipped around Freya's ankles. It made the flames in the hearth gutter. The door that had been closed now stood open. She didn't hesitate but made directly for the hallway. She entered the staff passageway. At the top of the steps, she was about to head down when she met Callum taking the final step up.

They stood for a moment at the top of the steps.

'Are you heading off now?' Callum asked.

Freya searched his eyes. 'I've been reminded in the last few days that opportunities in life should be grabbed,' she said. 'We shouldn't let them pass us by.'

'No,' Callum said, his voice soft. 'We shouldn't.' He shifted from one foot to the other. 'Last night,' he said. 'When we were talking over dinner, I didn't want to stop talking. There's something about you that made me say things.' He paused and smiled. 'I'm a rough tough Scotsman; we don't usually talk about our feelings.'

Freya laughed softly. 'When I touched your hand while you were picking up the wooden spoon, I didn't want to take my hand away.'

'Really?' Callum said with a smile.

'Really,' Freya said.

'I'm glad you felt like you had a Christmas last night,' Callum said.

Their hands were close and Callum brushed Freya's little finger with his.

'Tomorrow's the Epiphany,' Freya said. 'A time for making changes.' She took Callum's hand. He wrapped his fingers around hers.

Leading the way out into the hallway, Freya came to a stop beneath the ball wrapped in mistletoe. Music and laughter floated from the ballroom.

She turned to Callum.

'Is it good luck to kiss beneath a kissing bough?' she asked.

'It is,' Callum said.

Freya reached to put her arms around Callum's neck, and he wrapped his arms around her waist, pulling her close. They kissed and Freya felt Callum's lips and his touch in every part of her.

The guests in the ballroom clapped when a song came to an end.

Freya moved away from Callum. She looked up into his brown eyes. 'Happy Epiphany, Callum Miller,' she said.

'Happy Epiphany, Freya Harris,' Callum said.

He leant forward. They kissed again and Freya was sure she would never spend another Christmas alone.

A LETTER FROM THE AUTHOR

Dear reader,

Thank you so much for reading *A Twelfth Night Miracle*, I hope you enjoyed Freya's journey at Hill House. If you want to read more about the Mandevilles and their very special home, you can find them in the Mandeville Mystery series. If you want to join other readers in hearing all about my new releases and bonus content, you can sign up here:

www.stormpublishing.co/callie-langridge

If you enjoyed this book, it would be great if you could leave a review. Even a short review can make all the difference in encouraging a reader to discover my books for the first time. Thank you so much!

I have always loved Christmas and setting a time travel book in the festive season now and in the 1800s was a joy.

Thanks again for being part of this amazing journey with me and I hope you'll stay in touch – I have so many more stories and ideas to share with you.

Callie

instagram.com/CallieLangridge
facebook.com/CallieLangridgeAuthor
x.com/CLangridgeWrite

ACKNOWLEDGEMENTS

Sometimes life throws you a curve ball and you can tell your true supporters by how they respond. Thank you so much to Kathryn and Oliver at Storm for your understanding, patience and suggestions for this book. It has been a joy to work on it this year.

As ever, thank you to my band of fellow writers who are always there to cheer and celebrate. Thank you especially to Susie Lynes, Lisa Timoney, Claire McGlasson, Clarissa Angus, Emilie Olsson, Bev Thomas, Kate Riordan, Nicola Rayner and Zoe Antoniades.

Thank you to the best cheerleaders a writer could have – Kim, Tracy, Val and Virginia. And a special mention to Pete, my cheer-leader-in-chief x

RECIPES

When recipes appear in books, I am always tempted to give them a go, particularly if they are biscuits or cakes and even more so if they look simple to make.

Spices, dried fruit and perfumed waters feature heavily in recipes from the Regency period. Great examples of these are the rout cake and Shrewsbury cake. Without a doubt, they fall into the camp of being easy to make and delicious, particularly, if like me, you are a huge fan of rose-flavoured foods. I know this can be a contentious flavour profile, but give me a Turkish delight and I will likely be your friend forever!

Rout cakes take their name from routs – lively evening parties in the Regency period where these delicacies were served. A hostess would often be judged on the quality of the rout cake served at her gathering.

Shrewsbury cakes pre-date the Regency era but were very popular in the period. Named after the town in Shropshire, they are definitely a biscuit rather than a cake. Think spiced or citrusy thin shortbread and you are about there.

As with any historic bake, the recipes for these two treats have been adapted over the centuries, and each person who makes them will have their preference. If you don't fancy the alcohol, then feel free to increase more of the other liquids or add a little of your favourite citrus juice and zest. Oranges and lemons never go amiss in a Regency bake.

These recipes are modern interpretations of Regency treats, but if you want to try baking the cakes that Freya created for the Mandevilles and their guests at the Twelfth Night ball at Hill House, then they are a good starting point. If you are more adventurous, you could try making a Twelfth Night cake or marzipan (marchpane!) cake that Tristan would love, but they definitely do not fall into the simple to make camp!

Whatever you bake, enjoy.

Callie x

Rout cakes
(Makes roughly 20 cakes)

Ingredients
200g self-raising flour
100g butter
100g caster sugar
100g currants or sultanas or raisins – whichever you prefer or have in your cupboard
2 eggs
1 tbsp sweet sherry or brandy
1 tbsp freshly squeezed orange juice
1 tsp rosewater (you could substitute rose essence but use less)

Method

1. Sift your flour into a bowl, add the butter, and rub together using your fingers so that the mixture resembles fine breadcrumbs. (If you don't fancy getting your fingers in, this can be done in a processor. Equally, using the back of a fork to rub the ingredients together works in my experience.)

2. Add in whichever dried fruit you have chosen along with the sugar, and stir through the flour-and-butter breadcrumbs and give it a mix.

3. In a separate bowl, mix together all of your wet ingredients – eggs, sherry/brandy, orange juice, rosewater.

4. Gradually stir the egg mixture into the main bowl, adding a little of the egg mixture each time and stirring through the breadcrumbs.

5. Drop teaspoonfuls of the sticky, rough-looking mixture onto a greased baking tray. Be sure to leave space between each for the spread as they cook!

6. Bake at 180c for 10–12 minutes.

7. The cakes are ready when there is a slight golden colour on the peaks.

8. Remove from the oven and cool on racks.

9. These cakes can be stored in an airtight container if needed – but preferably enjoy immediately after they have cooled with a hot drink of your choice!

Shrewsbury cakes
(Makes roughly 20 biscuits)

Ingredients
100g butter (softened)
100g caster sugar
1 egg
200g plain flour
½ tsp cinnamon
½ tsp nutmeg
Zest of 1 lemon

1. Cream the butter and sugar together. One they are nicely combined, mix in the egg.

2. Sift the flour into the bowl and add the cinnamon and nutmeg. Stir it all together.

3. Add the lemon zest and stir again. You'll have to get your hands in now to bring it all together into a beautiful golden ball.

4. You should now have a nice firm dough, which you can roll out on a floured surface. About 5mm thick should do it.

5. Cut out the shapes with the cutter of your choice.

6. Place the shapes on a greased baking tray or a tray lined with baking paper and cook at 180c for roughly 12–18 minutes. The amount of cooking time will depend on the size of the cutter used.

7. Keep an eye on the biscuits as they cook. They should have a golden colour but no more.

8. Remove from the oven. Cool on a rack.

9. Serve on a delightful plate that makes you smile.

10. Eat and enjoy!

Printed in Dunstable, United Kingdom